HORRORFROST

HORRORFROST

Edward Newton

A
Grinning Skull Press
Publication
PO Box 67, Bridgewater, MA 02324

The Skull logo with stylized lettering was created for Grinning Skull Press by Dan Moran, http://dan-moran-art.com/.
Cover designed by Jeffrey Kosh, http://jeffreykosh.wix.com/jeffreykoshgraphics.

Published by Grinning Skull Press, P.O. Box 67, Bridgewater, MA 02324

ISBN-13: 978-1-947227-46-0 (paperback)
ISBN: 978-1-947227-47-7 (ebook)

DEDICATION

For Treina, Kobe, Gage, Oliver and Bennett

ACKNOWLEDGMENTS

Thank you to North Dakota, for a lifetime of research on snow and cold and white.

def. hoarfrost
hoar·frost
ˈhôr͵frôst/
noun
a grayish-white crystalline deposit of frozen water vapor formed in clear still weather on vegetation, fences, etc.

0°

Hoarfrost covers the glass in the small cabin, concealing the world outside. A fire licks the air inside, tasting the cold, snapping and snarling at the precipitous drop in temperature. A storm moves in, wind howling against the walls and whispering through the cracks and crevices of the old place. Snow falls from the sky in big, fat flakes, shushing and scraping against the pinewood logs of the foundation. It was just morning moments ago, but now darkness falls as the thick precipitation blots out the universe beyond.

Roman Carver doesn't even ponder the resort town at the bottom of the mountain slope, let alone the universe beyond it. Twenty years ago, he'd been a successful banker in a big city in the flattest part of Texas. In any given week, he could foreclose on a family home, bankrupt a small business, and deny loan after loan after loan, sending working folks into a financial spiral. He had been connected, corporate, and cold.

Then one day he unplugged. He stood up in the middle of an afternoon in December and walked to his floor-to-ceiling window in the corner office on the top floor of a downtown high-rise. It never snowed in this part of Texas, yet an errant snowflake drifted outside the plate glass, dancing like it did not have a care in the world. Roman had watched as it did some sort of natural ballet in the sky, a frosty kiss that broke a spell he had not even realized he was under.

There'd been a conference call playing on a speakerphone on his desk. His desk had been half the size of the room where he'd spent the past two decades of his life. He'd walked away from the desk, out of the room, and off the conference call without signing off, an urgent "Mister Carver? Mister Carver? Are you there?" following him all the way down the hall to the elevators. He'd owned a million dollar penthouse in the Renaissance district, but Roman did not even bother stopping at home before he left town forever. Six months into a relationship with a stockbroker from Austin, he never even bothered calling to tell her it was over.

Roman Carver had left Texas and came to the mountains of Montana.

He'd built this cabin with his own two hands. A man who had become successful entirely on his own, rising through the ranks to run a multimillion-dollar corporation, he had not asked for help on this new endeavor. Trial and error. His initial supplies had consisted of a flint lighter, some how-to books on survival, a first aid kit, a bowie knife, some tin pots and pans, fishing line and hooks, and a compound bow with complimentary arrows. The first month, he had almost starved. The first winter, he had almost froze. The first spring, he'd gotten so sick he thought he was going to die. That was all twenty years ago.

Roman is still alive.

He sips a mug of hot coffee cupped in calloused hands. Steam issues off the black surface, further obscuring the view out the window. Not that he needs to see snow. This high in the mountains, a storm could easily yield a foot of new powder overnight. Nothing to do but hunker down and wait out the worst. He stares at the fire. There is no electricity in the cabin. No television. No phone. No electronics of any kind. Roman had left it all behind.

A noise outside sounds like a tree giving under a load of snow, the burden beating the ground with a solid thump. The surface of the coffee in his mug ripples like a pond disturbed by a pebble. Roman had not seen a movie in twenty years, but he knew *Jurassic Park*. He is fairly sure he does not have to worry about a t-rex, but the rippled-java effect was certainly not caused by falling snow. Nothing short of an avalanche.

"The hell?" he mumbles, his voice dry and scratchy from irregular use.

Roman has not gone down to the town in the two decades since he arrived from Texas. He did not need supplies. No news. No gossip. He crossed paths with an occasional hiker in the warm months and a skier every once in a while during the winter, but he never stopped for more than a "Howdy-do." When he had come up into the mountains, Bill Clinton had been president, Elway had gotten his Super Bowl ring, and "Mmmbop" had been driving him crazy. He never asked what happened after that.

No one ever comes up here in anything big enough to cause a noise like that. Roman glares at the opaque pane. *What is out there?* He ponders for a while until curiosity finally outweighs the cold.

His coat is bearskin, a grizzly he'd taken ten years ago. Boots are sheepskin. Gloves rabbit. Before he'd left Texas, he'd been a regular contributor to PETA, and now he looked like some creature the organization would seek to protect. Ethical treatment of animals is using every part of the kill, the spirit of the beasts living on by helping Roman survive. He had never had such respect for the creatures of the wild when he'd been using them as a charitable tax deduction.

Maybe it was an animal that made the noise? A moose that bumped into a nearby tree?

Roman opens the front door and a small hill of snow crumbles into the cabin. He pushes through a drift as high as his waist, then pulls the door shut behind him. The wind cuts as sharp as the knife strapped to his waist, ready in case some winter-starved predator dares attack. The white is absolute, the driven snow like a wall that might be solid but for the shifting grains moving before his eyes.

He pushes through the snow. The cabin is in a clearing, and his home disappears behind him after he takes just three steps. He knows these woods like the back of his hand in the dark, but the blowing snow is disorienting. Better off blind than mesmerized, Roman closes his eyes and forges forward. He marks his way by putting a hand on the old tree ten yards from his front door. From there, the denser forest blocks some of the blizzard.

Roman moves in the direction of the sound, forward, forward, until he finds what he is looking for. It is a blue spruce, snapped in two, as big as any other tree in the woods. Boughs heavy with the season's snow must have sounded like an earthquake when it broke. But the weight of the snow could not have made the tree trunk crack in half. Something broke it off. Something big enough to snap it mid-section, some sixty feet up.

"The hell?" Roman says again, the wind whiting out his words.

A gust brings snowy blindness, suddenly obscuring everything. Whatever did this is still out there somewhere, in the white. Did a small plane crash in the woods? There is no other evidence. A meteor? Maybe. Something else? Something else covers a lot of possibilities. Roman has largely ignored the developments of the modern world these last two decades, so maybe they had invented something that could do this kind of damage. After all, man is always inventing new ways to destroy nature.

Another trembling bass, this one thrumming through the soles of Roman's sheepskin boots. Like an explosion deep within the earth, but the sound carries across the winter air, muffled by the thick snow. The origin is back the way he came, from the direction of his cabin.

Roman stares into the white before rushing off. Deliberating. He knows the dangers of this world. He has crossed every type of animal that lives in these mountains over the last two decades, sometimes as predator, sometimes as prey, sometimes as passerby. It feels like something else. There is something else on his mountain. Something new. But he cannot see anything through the snowfall, just a shifting white curtain that conceals everything beyond.

Roman moves back toward his home. He gets to the old tree and stops again, eyes straining against the static of the snowstorm. He cannot pick out a stationary object within all the turgid swirl of the scene. No hint. Nothing he can separate from the constant white noise.

He can't see anything out in the clearing. The blowing snow erases everything. He steps forward, one foot in front of the other. The clearing is about fifty yards in diameter, his cabin at the center. If he loses his way in the disorienting blizzard, he will find more trees. Another step. The snow gathers in drifts now nearly to his shoulders. Forward, forward, forward. Right to his front door.

Or where his front door ought to be.

The walls are all flat, smashed to the ground and nearly covered already by fresh snow. Everything he ever had has been pummeled, flat as the pancakes he made just that morning.

Something squashed the cabin as easily as Roman might flatten a pill bug under his heel.

Whatever it was could be as close as his fingertips, concealed by the white.

And the wind rises, the temperature slips another degree, and Roman Carver shivers.

It has nothing to do with the cold.

-1°

Trevin Mendoza sits on the edge of the bed. Behind him, a tussle of pink hair peeks out from beneath a rumpled bed sheet. The head does not belong to his fiancé. It is someone who had been just a friend before last night. Trevin watches the ice creep up and across the glass of the patio door that leads to the suite's balcony. It is cold outside. It is cold inside.

Maybe he is not ready to be married. That's what Alex had told him last night, before things got out of hand and went too far. Those words had made sense a few hours ago. Glancing back at Alex's pink bangs sticking out from the tangled bedding, they still make sense. His mother had always told him he wasn't the marrying kind. He hates to admit his mother is right about anything, but the evidence still hangs in the air like Alex's musky aftershave.

This is supposed to be a bachelor party weekend. The engaged couple came to Enchanted Point Ski Resort together, with an entourage, ready to celebrate the last days of bachelorhood before tying the knot in Vegas next week. Alex is supposed to be the best man at the ceremony. Yet somehow Alex had ended up in Trevin's bed. And bad things had ensued.

Such deliciously bad things.

Shit.

Trevin stands up, considers pants, then snorts. What goddamn difference did it make now? He walks naked to the icy patio door and peeks out the small corner not yet covered with frost. Outside, snow blankets the small town of Zukunft Falls, Montana. From what Trevin can see of the balcony, the railings look like lumps under a sheet. Like a lover concealed beneath the blanket of sin.

Trevin sighs. The breath turns to condensation on the glass, then freezes, crackled ice radiating out from the edges of the pane toward the center. It looks like broken glass. One more broken thing. He turns away.

Alex is sitting up in bed, watching him.

"You look like someone caught you with your hand in the cookie jar, Trev," Alex says.

"Don't call me that," Trevin says. "Only David calls me that."

"I bet he might call you something else when you tell him about this."

"Who says I am going to tell him?" Trevin challenges. "It would ruin everything."

"The only reason you did this is so you can tell him. You *want* to ruin everything."

Trevin looks away. Modesty has never been part of his personality, but standing here naked in front of Alex, he feels ashamed. Alex is right. He did this so that there could be no turning back. If he simply told David that he did not want to get married, David would try to talk him out of it. David would succeed in talking him out of it. But this?

There is no talking out of this.

"You want me to tell him?" Alex asks.

Trevin glares. Passions can flare between two people, dangerous emotions both dark and bright. So often the extremes occur on opposite sides of night.

"I'll tell him," Trevin says.

"When?"

"Tomorrow," Trevin responds, postponing the inevitable.

One last day together.

Trevin and David have been a couple for more than four years, ever since they'd met online shortly after David moved to L.A. from Nebraska. He'd been an ingenue, and Trevin was a seasoned SoCal social superman. Trevin had introduced David to everything fantastic, and David had showed him what it meant to take a step back and appreciate those fantastic things.

David had told him on their fourth anniversary that he wanted to move forward or he was going to move on. Trevin proposed. And for a while it had been fine. Exciting. A new adventure. But then they'd started planning this trip and reality started to solidify. It got hard to see the future. Then it started to show cracks.

Now, it is in pieces.

"Why wait 'til tomorrow?" Alex presses.

"Tomorrow is as good as today."

"That is the thing about tomorrows, Trev. They never get here."

"Get dressed," Trevin snaps. "Get out."

Last night they couldn't get enough of each other. Now Trevin has had enough. This is the other side of the coin.

Somewhere outside the translucent window, the world gray and gloomy despite the midmorning hour, comes the sound of thunder. Alex, pants up and shirt half-buttoned, turns to the patio door. Trevin, still without a stitch on, approaches the balcony. Another boom. Louder. Closer.

"What was that?" Alex asks.

Trevin steps into a pair of Calvin Klein sweatpants that were crumpled in a corner. He pulls on the white and blue Bogner ski jacket he wore on the slopes yesterday. There are a pair of Hestra mittens that must be Alex's tossed not far from pink bikini briefs that also do not belong to Trevin. He pulls on the mittens. Stepping into his ski boots, he opens the glass door; the quick flick of cold takes his breath. Yesterday had been sunny and perfect; this morning is like nothing a SoCal surfer has ever seen. Trevin likes his water in waves instead of flakes.

The white is absolute. He remembers seeing the white sand of

Coronado Beach for the first time and telling his boyfriend at the time that it must be like walking in snow. Nope. It is nothing like snow. This is endless, oppressive, unstoppable. Trevin feels like he is staring into oblivion, and if he looks into it long enough, he might go blind.

Somewhere in the white, another boom. Trevin cannot be sure with the swirls and eddies of the snow, but he thinks the sound made the flakes *vibrate*.

"That is not thunder," Alex says from right beside him, making Trevin jump. "It sounded like an explosion."

Alex had donned a pair of spare gloves, hat, ski goggles, as well as his own jacket and boots. He looks ready to survive a blizzard. Well, if he wasn't going to leave willingly by the main hotel room door...

"Go check it out," Trevin goads.

Alex gives him a face. "Why don't you go?"

"You're dressed for it," Trevin says. "Goggles and everything. I wouldn't be able to see a thing out there in that blizzard."

They stare out into the suffocating snow. The wind gusts and Trevin cannot see more than two feet in front of him. For one ex-cruciating moment, he imagines David, unseen, in front of him, looking back as Trevin looks out, yet they cannot see each other. Close enough to reach out and touch, yet separated by an insurmount-able distance. The space between them is too great to erase.

"Scared?" Trevin taunts.

Another boom.

"Yes," Alex says.

Instead of forward, both men take a step back. Retreat. They close the frosted door and stare at the pane veiled with hoarfrost. Snow had sneaked in while they'd been staring down the storm, tendrils like ten-tacles winding away from the closed door, quickly melting, fingers of water leaving wet streaks on the gray carpet. Outside, the sounds of more explosions, like someone had declared war on this resort town.

Then the lights go out.

-2°

Rhonda Phelps stares into the mirror. Was that another wrinkle? Another line? Shitshitshit. They popped up lately like weeds in a garden. Every morning. Festering like an infection. Of course, the stress over each one likely caused the next, a snowball rolling down a hill gathering momentum. Her mama, God rest her soul, might hate her for it, but Rhonda plans on going under the knife as soon as she gets back to Rochester.

She had dyed her hair for the occasion, a professional job that she'd driven an hour out of town to get done, far enough away from anyone who might have known her. She has been doing the same thing since the first errant strand of gray arrived some fifteen years ago. She had her regular local hairstylist, and then her secret one, who existed out of town, for coloring, like she was married to one and cheating with the other. All to keep up the illusion. Everything to stave off the realization of time running out.

This trip was a bust. She had been dating Howard online for the last few months. They arranged a face-to-face for a week of skiing in the middle of nowhere, Montana. They'd met for the first time ever in the lobby of the community lodge to kick off the vacation with some drinks and an introductory meeting. Well, Howard's online profile picture was from a good fifty pounds ago. And as he had pointed out before leaving for home five days early, Rhonda's was from a good two decades ago.

She had lied about her age. She has been lying about her age since forty snuck up and stole her future. For a few years, it had been easy to get away with. Perpetually thirty-nine, she looked it until just recently. Something had changed in the last year. Like the borrowed time she had used up on lying these last ten years had all piled on at once, advancing too fast. The woman in the mirror is not thirty-nine. Tomorrow, Rhonda turns fifty.

He had left her the birthday gift he'd brought. It is a gray scarf the color of hoarfrost. She picks it up now and wraps it around her neck. It covers up some of the waddles and wrinkles that seemed to appear overnight. Like her body knows fifty is only a day away.

There is another reverberating bass in the distance, like a drumbeat loud enough to make her bones ache. Thunder? Some local phenomenon? An artificial annoyance?

The old woman in the mirror disappears into darkness as the lights flicker and fail. Like candles blown out on a birthday cake.

Howard had left, but Rhonda had decided to stay. The suite is prepaid through the end of the week, and she was not prepared to go home to New York and face her family and friends about the shitty reality of her romantic vacation. Certainly, Sheila would arrange a night out with the gang for Rhonda's birthday. None of them believed she was still thirty-nine. That had turned from a cute joke to an awkward obliviousness over the last couple of years. No one would be surprised she is turning fifty.

None of them except Rhonda herself.

She had such plans. She had wanted to be married by thirty, two kids by thirty-five, and by now she had expected to be cheering at a high school football game or giving a standing ovation at the state spelling bee. Instead, she looks like a grandmother with no grandchildren to show for it.

The dark is a brief blessing.

Then she feels her way out of the suite. Dim light leaks in from the terrace doors flecked with crystalline frost, a gray ambiance that reminds her of the strands that populate her black hair, more and more and more. Before she had her coif colored for this trip, she'd plucked enough gray weeds to make Barbie's granny a wig.

The light is just bright enough to separate objects from the pathway, barely illuminating the route to the front door of the suite. Rhonda opens the door with the number 438 on the front. In the hall, emergency lights cast everything in a dull red glow. Other occupants stand in doorways and gather in small groups.

"What's going on?" Rhonda asks a woman who looks like she is maybe twenty-five and does not have to lie about her age. Little blonde thing with hair all tussled like she just woke up and still looks as pretty as if she spent hours on her face. The girl obviously exited her suite without putting on a bra, the nip in the air ensuring it is not the only nip noticeable. What is not noticeable is any sag whatsoever.

Little bitch.

"The lights are out," the girl answers, like Rhonda had just asked the stupidest question ever. She does not even look up from the phone she is on, texting away like some stenographer transcribing their conversation. The blonde did not have to ask anyone in the hall what is happening; her phone is the only companion she needs.

Someone ought to slap some sense into the girl, but that someone is not Rhonda. Not today. Instead, she turns away from the nubile youth and walks across the room to a woman who makes Rhonda look young in comparison.

The occupant in the room across from Rhonda's looks like she is in her sixties, a slight, sprightly white woman wringing her hands like she is applying lotions and pissed about it. She is wearing colorful leggings over a fit form and a sweater that looks as trendy as anything the idiot blonde might wear. The older woman at least has the sense to wear undergarments.

Closer now, Rhonda notices the sweater is on backward. Under other circumstances, Rhonda would have honored the sisterhood code and notified the lady—Rhonda is not shy about boogers hanging from noses or a piece of spinach caught in someone's teeth—but there seems to be something more important to discuss than turned-around tops.

"Do you know what's happening?" Rhonda asks.

"No," the woman answers with a worried expression, not wasting words with a stupid reply. "Clarice went down to the lobby. She was concerned after the explosions started. No nonsense, that one. She scooted off before the lights went dark. I hope she isn't stuck in the elevator. With her arthritis, she never takes the stairs. Do you think they have an emergency backup for the elevators?"

"I'm sure they do, ma'am," Rhonda replies. She has no idea.

Someone with a flashlight sweeping the hall left to right starts coming down the corridor. It is a resort employee with a name tag that says "Conner." Conner looks the same age as the blonde still standing braless in the doorway of her suite, the glow of her phone casting shadows across her shirt, highlighting twin nubs that keep getting pointier. Conner gets an eyeful, pausing right between Rhonda and the girl.

"You have some answers for us, Conner?" Rhonda asks.

"Just stay inside your suite, ma'am," he answers without looking at Rhonda, absorbing an eyeful of the blonde's perky bosom.

It's like Rhonda isn't even there. Age has made her invisible. There had been a time when she'd been the one who had caught the boys' attention. Now, she is the incessant buzz in the background.

"Have you seen my friend?" the old woman asks Conner. "Her name is Clarice Otter. She went down to your lobby to find out what this is all about."

"What?" Conner stutters, distracted by delectable tits. Then he finally turns, the task at hand finally resurfacing. He looks at the old woman. "I didn't see anyone on my way up. She might still be in the lobby. She shouldn't be wandering around without a flashlight."

"Why did the lights go out?" Rhonda asks.

Conner looks as clueless as the blonde across the hallway. "For your own safety, please return to your suite until the electricity comes back on." He is reciting the company line, like an automated message repeating on an intercom.

Another explosion sounds outside. Closer. The maid's cart parked under the emergency light two doors down rolls a few inches up the hall from the reverberation, a bottle of cleaner shaking off the edge of the cart. Rhonda grabs the door jamb to steady herself, her other hand cupping the old woman's elbow to make sure the senior citizen does not topple over.

"What the fuck is that?" Conner swears, eschewing company protocol in favor of stark fear.

The blonde looks up from the glowing screen of her phone like she has just witnessed someone murdered right in front of her face. "I lost my signal."

Conner pulls his own electronic device from the pocket of his resort uniform. "Me, too." In the pale light from his screen, he looks like a ghost. "The tower must be down."

"No Wi-Fi, either," the blonde adds.

Another explosion shakes the entire building.

"My last message," Conner whispers, reading, professional mission now entirely abandoned. "It's from my buddy who works out at the lifts, up the mountain. He says there is something in the snow."

Rhonda looks over Conner's shoulder and reads the last text message on his screen from someone called "Doobie," a dubious eyewitness account from someone named after a marijuana cigarette: "cant see it jist shadows theirs somethng trrble in the white."

The bass sounds again, this time shaking Rhonda so hard she stumbles forward, almost knocking into Miss Braless Blondie. *There's something terrible in the white.* For so long, she has dreaded turning fifty. Wished tomorrow would never come. But now, Rhonda Phelps wants nothing more than to see just one more day.

-3°

I'm in a bad place.

I'm in a very bad place.

In the basement of the Enchanted Point Ski Resort, Zakaria Alaoui has a little area all to himself. When the building was originally opened, the resort was heated by great boilers that pumped hot water into pipes in the walls and throughout the hotel. There are great cast iron tubs in the lower level, each weighing a couple of tons, metal behemoths that have pipes both great and small extending out in every direction. The vats are huge and hideous. When the resort installed modern furnaces years ago, the old tanks were too expensive to break up and haul out of the basement, so the remodelers simply placed the new units directly in front of the old boilers.

One of the tremendous vats bordering Zack's hideaway has an access panel that looks like a door from a submarine or a spaceship. It stands open, like an invitation to the dark. There is a spoked wheel in the middle of the door that would lock it, and moldered seals around the perimeter. At some point, the panel was used to gain entry into the tank for inspections when the boiler was drained. Now it is a doorway into nothingness. Zack stares into the abyss sometimes, but he has never gone inside. He has never shined a light into it because he is afraid there is nothing to see. It seems like a crypt.

One of the tanks moans. It happens when it is windy since the ends of some of the nest of pipes extend out into the world, still uncapped. The sound is like someone in great pain dying.

Zack stares at the dark opening. He shivers.

When Zack and his mother had moved into the employee rooms at the rear of the resort, Zack was only eight and still infinitely curious about all the things he did not know. He'd explored the hotel from top to bottom and found the alcove behind the new furnaces nestled amongst the great iron vats of old. Someone had previously commandeered the area for a hideaway, stocking the little space between the tomblike tubs with a shabby sofa, two tables, a shelf of musty books, and a power cord spliced into the resort's backup generator. No one had been there for a long time by the time Zack had found it. Whoever had originally furnished the hideaway was gone. So now it belongs to Zack. Only Zack.

It was once a good place to hide. Now it is the perfect place to die.

I'm in a bad place, and there is only one way out.

How long will his mom search for his body? Eventually, he would start to stink. Obese and unhealthy, the smell might come sooner rather than later. It would be the only clue. Zack didn't like to think about that. He did not want to wonder what would happen to his fat, ugly body after he is gone. After it is over. That is someone else's mess to clean up. His mother is a maid at the resort. She is used to cleaning up after other people.

The great tank beside Zack makes its noise, deeper this time, as if the end is nigh. The school bus driver had hit a goat on a field trip one spring, and the bleating noise it made in its suffering was a quieter version of the reverberation of the cast iron vat. The driver took the goat by the horns as it lay suffering and twisted and put the animal out of its misery. Sometimes an end is better than just going on and on and on.

There is always one way out of any bad place.

Zack brings up the last post on his phone. He does not get a signal down here behind concrete and steel, so the last screen he opened is still showing on his device. Why does he even have a social media account of any kind? It is just an open door for insults. But some people also post encouraging words. His aunt in Morocco always has a kind expression, but then again she has never met Zack in person. Strangers can afford to be caring. It is the people he knows who manage the worst kinds of hate.

The post that sent him to the bowels of the resort came from Dot Kahn. Everyone thinks Dot is so cool in high school, but when Zack was eight and had arrived in this new town, he'd known her as Dorothy. Dorothy was a chubby girl with glasses two sizes too big and prone to nose-picking. But one summer in middle school, her mother sent her to her grandparents' home in Missoula, and when she came back three months later, she was thinner, taller, fingers outside nostril, new contact lenses, and calling herself Dot. Dot Kahn is cool.

She probably doesn't even remember that Zack is one of her social media "friends" that sees all her posts. While she certainly did not have time for outcasts like Zack Alaoui anymore, she is not prone to wanton cruelty. She probably forgot he is even amongst the hundreds of members of the group that follows her profile.

He reads the post again: "The Gurp asked out Mandy Ryder to the Frost Festival. Gross!"

I am in such a very, very bad place.

The Gurp. The name came from one terrible moment in eighth grade in the lunchroom. Zack's mother had packed him a soda. The school lunches were all about healthy choices, but his mom had said choices didn't always have to be healthy. So he sat alone at his regular table with a bottle of cola and three PBJs. He drank too much and too long because Mandy Ryder walked by and he was distracted by her pink skirt sashaying like a pocket watch, back and forth, back and forth, hypnotizing him. When he put down the soda bottle, it was half empty. Carbonation bubbled in his guts. He worried half his PBJ was coming up with a belch. But in the end, it was mostly air, a great bellow that sorta sounded like someone violently vomiting, so loud it made even the adults at the teachers' table turn their heads. "What a gross burp," someone said. "It was like a Gurp!" And the name stuck ever after.

Dot Kahn with her damned cool name maybe does not even remember that the Zakaria Alaoui on her long list of online acquaintances is the one she now calls the Gurp. Dot had taught Zack how to play chess when she'd been just Dorothy, and they would watch SpongeBob for hours at a time. He hopes she does not feel guilty about her part in his untimely end. If there is any Dorothy left in there, Zack supposes she will.

The tank ten feet away makes an awful noise, a gurp of its own, deeper and more menacing than the low moan more characteristic of its usual tone. There is no bus driver around to put the decommissioned cauldron out of its misery. Besides, the sound is less wounded and more menacing. Like a warning. Zack stares into the black eye of the boiler's open door, but there is no light in the darkness.

Maybe God is telling me to come back from this very bad place?

God had His chance. Too fucking late.

Zack taps on his smart screen. No Wi-Fi here in the bowels of the world. No cell signal in the dungeon of the resort. So whatever he writes and sends will be suspended until someone finds his phone and brings it back to civilization. Once the devices come back online, it will post his last words. His suicide note. For all the world to see. He tucks the phone in his back pocket, a new-age kind of note for these sorts of things.

The gun had been here when Zack first found this place. Maybe whoever had furnished this hideaway had been in a bad place, too. Maybe that was why they left without taking anything away. Whoever it was might have found another way to die, up in the real world, where things were both brighter and darker. They did not need to die in the basement.

The Gurp deserves to die right here. Right now.

Zack looks at the gun sitting on the small table. It was dusty when he found it, but he has cleaned it since. Checked the chamber for bullets. Everything is in order and looks like it will work. It only has to work once. Zack picks it up, curls a finger around the trigger.

A bad place.

The tank makes another sound, a low hum, like electricity moving through wires overhead. The sound gets louder and louder. Zack stands up, walking to one of the massive tanks. He stops beside the open door, the absolute pitch within as cold and endless as Zack's future. With the hand not grasping a gun, he puts his palm against the rough iron side. The surface vibrates, like a tuning fork from physics class. The sound gets louder and louder and louder. Deafening. Zack winces.

Then the roof caves in on the bad place, and there is no place at all.

-4°

Esther Williams wanders the hallway of the Enchanted Point Ski Resort. She looks for her friend. Clarice Otter had gone down to the lobby to find out what is going on. She hadn't come back. So Esther is going to find her.

It is snowing inside. There are drifts all along the corridor down to where the elevator should be at the end. The wind whips along the hallway, making piles to each side against the walls. The missing door between rooms 418 and 414 opens out into a blinding blizzard. Stinging pellets pepper Esther as she shuffles past a precipitous drop-off.

The attendant at the front desk when they checked in had asked if they wanted to stay in the northeast wing or the south wing. The northeast wing afforded a lovely view of the valley down the mountain, white sloping all the way down to a picturesque village at the base of Bailey's Peak. The south wing looked toward the top of the mountain, which the clerk warned was usually cloaked in cloud cover. Then she added, "But when the skies clear enough to see the peak, oh what a sight!"

Esther stops in the middle of the corridor. The last door on her right is 407. The elevators at the end where Clarice and Esther came up to the fourth floor are gone. The emergency staircase that was located across from the elevators is gone. Rooms 401 through 406 are gone. The hallway more than two feet in front of her is gone.

She stops at the edge and stares into the white. Esther cannot see more than a few inches in front of her face, but she knows what is beyond. Nothing. The rest of the south wing has been ripped away. If the wind would cease and the skies open, she could stand right here in the hall and get a perfect view of the peak, "oh what a sight."

The lobby is gone. The rest of the hotel that should extend to the central pillar where the elevators used to be located is gone. The northeast wing ought to be on Esther's right, but there is only white, the wind and snow uninhibited by walls. Clarice is supposed to be in the lobby, checking to see what is going on with the *boom-boom-boom* sounds coming from the blizzard. Now Clarice is gone.

Esther realizes her hands are freezing. The wind chill is lethal, and she is still wearing only the sweater she got from her son's new wife (What's-her-name) just for the trip to the mountains and leggings that looked like tubular rainbows that Clarice Otter had talked her into (Clarice had said she thought Esther would look just *darling* on the slopes this week.) The wind cuts through the meek defenses like an X-Acto knife through felt, slicing shapes from things without form. She feels like the snow is mirroring her thoughts, and her thoughts are just static and noise. Until she snaps out of it.

Now she shivers.

Esther looks back, and the blizzard has obscured the distance *inside* the hotel. Sure, the hallway ended in a drop off that would be the end of anyone who wasn't watching their step, and behind is just snowsnowsnow. And sure, she walked by room 416 where the door was missing and looked out into the endless white. But those were exits leading to the outside (even if they'd been interior passageways just a little while ago). The hallway back to her own room is *inside*. So it is odd that there are snowbanks three feet high piled along the walls.

Before he died, Esther's husband, Jerome, had gone through a midlife crisis. It had been later than midlife, occurring in his late fifties. Actually, his midlife would have been about thirty, as he had died just before he turned sixty. His rebellion had been mild. He had started going to the gym and joined a Zumba class. He had worn jeans instead of slacks for the first time in his life. And Jerome had purchased a convertible he named Tammy, and he made lewd jokes about taking Tammy's top down.

He had treated Tammy more like a baby than a lady. Washed her each sunny day. Checked the oil and the air in the tires every time before he drove her. Jerome wouldn't let anyone ride in Tammy if they had had so much as a crumb of food anywhere on their person. And he had never, ever, never left Tammy's top down in the rain.

Someone had left the top down on the Enchanted Point Ski Resort, and now it is snowing inside.

Esther shuffles through the snow. Such a curious effect. She imagines it will ruin the carpet when it melts. What a flood! She rubs her hands together to keep them warm as she moves slowly along the hallway, back the way she came. If the roof is gone, where can she go for shelter? Her room would not have a roof either. And there is no staircase to descend to a lower floor, where this floor would at least act as the ceiling. No way out. Like being stuck on a rooftop during a snowstorm. How very curious, indeed.

"What are you doing out here, ma'am?" comes a concerned voice from the white in front of her, through the snow falling in the hall.

It is the woman who had spoken to Esther earlier, when the electricity first winked out and the whining blonde across the hall complained about the Wi-Fi being down. At least there had been a roof. Not long after, the phones became just hi-tech flashlights, and the roof was gone. And the stairs and elevators. And the northeast wing. And Clarice Otter.

The woman has gone gray. Not her hair, which is obviously dyed to disguise her true age. Not her skin, which is still black and shines in the white. Not her eyes, chestnut and fierce. It is her aura, the projection of who she is. Before, when she asked Esther if she knew what was happening and called her "ma'am," the woman had been successful in appearing half her age. Now the years are piled onto her face, fifty years of fear etched into her expression.

"I am trying to find Clarice," Esther says.

The woman looks over Esther's shoulder into the blizzard blowing along the corridor. "There is no going that way."

Esther scowls. "You don't think I know that? I am not some clueless toddler! The stairs are gone. So are the elevators."

"This way," the woman decides, taking Esther by the hand and leading her away from the dead end. Her hand is warm and steady and serves to calm Esther's incessant chills. "We'll find another way down. We can get to another stairway and get to the ground. We'll find Clarice after we—"

"Clarice is dead," Esther declares.

"You don't know that," the stranger says.

Esther does not cry. She doesn't even feel sad. She only feels cold. So as the woman drags her back, past the room she had shared with Clarice, and goes south along the long corridor, Esther follows. The roof is missing all the way to a bend in the hotel. There are others, wandering before them single file like they are in line at the DMV. They join the end of the line.

"My name is Rhonda Phelps," the woman offers, extending a hand.

"Esther Williams," Ester replies. "Like the swimmer. Only not as famous."

Rhonda looks at her with puzzlement overlaying her terror. She did not know either Esther. Neither Williams is so famous anymore. Rhonda might be older than she once looked, and now she looks older than she is, but either way, she is not old enough to remember the original Esther Williams.

There is a staircase at the end of the hall. The roof and the whole side of the building have been torn away, like a Barbie house that folds out from the middle. The guests of the hotel descend one by one, carefully navigating steps slick with snow and ice. The line moves slowly because to rush would mean a pile-up akin to traffic crashing on a busy interstate.

The loud boom sounds again, shaking the snowy length of hallway, making the people on the stairs steady themselves against the walls. Esther and Rhonda, still two dozen guests back away from the stairs, both look up into the impenetrable white.

"When I was a child and it would storm, my gran always told me a story from her homeland, from when she was a child back in Nigeria," Rhonda says, to stave off fear and mitigate shock. "She told me *Amadioha* is the god of justice and uses his powers over thunder and lightning to judge the wicked. She would say, '*Amadioha magbukwa gi*.' Amadioha will punish you. I don't know if she meant it to make me feel better or worse, but when I was little and did something bad, a part of me always expected a roll of thunder."

Another rumble, so close to the last, nearer than the previous one.

"I don't think that noise has anything to do with any god, dear," Esther replies.

Rhonda nods.

Rhonda might be a lot older than she wants to appear, but she is still young and strong where Esther is unsteady. They make their way down the stairwell carefully but efficiently. Others had arrived after them from rooms on the fourth floor, coming down single file behind Esther and Rhonda. Guests from the third and second floors merge with the people from the fourth at each landing, everyone exiting in an orderly fashion. As if the situation is too bizarre for panic. Shock and cold have rendered the collective bunch, who are moving along like automatons, nearly catatonic.

Esther and Rhonda arrive on the first floor, and Rhonda exhales like they have just successfully crossed a tightrope. A plume of frost hangs in front of her face. Esther looks up like she does not recognize the levels of the resort overhead. She blinks rapidly, then looks away, rubbing her hands together like she is lathering soap. She looks toward the place where the lobby used to be.

"Now," Esther declares determinedly, "I need to find where Clarice has run off to."

She looks at her new friend, What's-her-name, and the woman looks back with a sad expression. And Esther does not know why.

-5°

Xueman Wang had a recurring nightmare about her daughter, Aspen. She was searching, calling out her name in a world filled with fog. Nothing was defined, just shapes that might be Aspen swirling in the mist, or they might be complete strangers or something dangerous. The fog muffled her voice, and she couldn't move faster than a slow shuffle in any direction for fear of running into a wall or stumbling off a cliff. Her daughter could be five feet away or five hundred miles, but Xueman couldn't see. Aspen was lost, and Xueman could not find her.

She awoke, always, with a scream stuck in her throat.

Now Xueman wonders if it was less dream and more premonition.

She tunes out the panicked chant in her mind: *What happened? What happened? What happened?* Picking through the rubble, she cannot fathom the disaster. She can only search and pray and hope. There isn't room for any other thoughts or she would break down in tears, crushed, despondent, and wrecked. Xueman ignores the impossibility all around her and focuses on the one real thing that matters: Aspen is missing.

Why did she go out? Because of a stupid craving? She went her first forty years without smoking a single cigarette, but she stupidly started at an advanced age. Her stress level had just been too high. It had begun late last summer, before Aspen's fall semester started. A senior in high school. Just a year before she was gone. Xueman couldn't handle losing her baby. Accepted to MIT, Aspen would be moving across the country come August. So she had started smoking.

They make you work to slowly kill yourself. The "approved" smoking areas were situated far away from civilization, as if smokers were lepers who cannot be allowed too near the rest of the population for fear of contamination. So Xueman had huddled with other desperate addicts, enduring snow and cold and wind against all logic, just for a quick fix.

The first *boom* had sounded before she even arrived at the designated smoking area. It had not stopped her trek to tobacco nirvana. Loud. Big. Sonic boom? Demolition?

The second explosion had occurred as Xueman was lighting up.

"What the hell was that?" a thin black man who looked like he might blow away in a strong gust had asked. The blizzard obscured him whenever the wind gusted around them.

"Thundersnow," a large woman in a blue parka had answered, the smoke issuing from her mouth and the snow making her a chimera, not white nor black nor any other color.

"That's something else," an ancient woman puffing on a home-rolled stick had croaked. They say that smoking kills, but the senior citizen looked like she was somewhere around a hundred. Apparently, it does not kill everyone.

Another boom had sounded halfway through Xueman's cigarette. Then another as she squashed her butt in the proper receptacle. The woman in the blue parka tossed her own butt into a big snow bank. Xueman scowled and started off in the opposite direction.

The pathway to and from the designated smoking area is bordered by an iron railing, and Xueman wondered if it is for the sole purpose of preventing anyone from wandering off into the white and getting lost in a blizzard. To lose your way out in a snowstorm would be certain death. The path led to safety.

Back to shelter from the blizzard.

Another thunderclap sounded so loudly it shook the ground and knocked Xueman on her bottom.

And then the world had exploded in front of her.

Gas had ignited here and there, bright balls of fire making a misty light show dozens of feet in the air. Through the shadow of snow, Xueman had seen sections of the hotel's walls come down; huge chunks of the resort had sailed through the curtain of white, and the entirety of the roof had pinwheeled down the mountain to her left, making the world shake and the snowfall quake.

It was Armageddon.

It had lasted for several long seconds.

Then silence. The snowfall had muted the aftershocks of destruction. The world had fallen quiet, as if everything beyond had been erased and Xueman was the only thing left in all existence.

She had scrambled to her feet and rushed forward, with just one thought on her mind: *Aspen*!

Now she sees the northeast wing, and it looks like a wrecking ball had worked it over. Yet the destruction had happened in mere moments. Instead of debris and devastation, the site is entirely razed. Xueman recognizes the marble floor that tiled the lobby from when they checked in. Now the front desk is gone, along with the walls and roof. Xueman stands in a squalor of snow where moments ago had been a four-story building. Gone. Just gone.

She looks around; it is white in every direction. Something and nothing wherever she turns. The room she shared with Aspen had been to her right, and the only thing she sees now is sifting, shifting snow. White on white.

"Aspen!"

The sound is like screaming into a pillow. No one beyond a few feet could hear her. Xueman moves forward, toward the place she left her daughter.

Something massive looms in the white, leaning over her like a giant stooping to see the ants. As she steps forward, the snow disappears a bit. What is left of the hotel rises before her, blocking the wind. The building has been ripped down the middle, a dozen rooms exposed like an architectural elevation in real life. Severed pipes leak water, little waterfalls that steam in the cold. Xueman can see inside so many rooms. She has a hard time deciding which, if any, is hers.

A howl, like a wolf, or someone in the throes of great pain. The wind whips sound in every direction, so it is behind her, beside her, everywhere and nowhere. In the distance, another *boom*, and Xueman pauses. Is the howl a warning rather than a call for help?

The white whispers. *Runrunrunrunrun.*

The wind erases everything again, the hotel gone right before her eyes. Swirling in a flurry of flakes, the world becomes nothing. The wounded howl slithers through the snow, a soprano undertone to the whistling wind. It could be Aspen. It could be anything.

Xueman picks a direction and pushes into the white.

She finds him in a pile of snow, writhing like a werewolf in mid transformation. Xueman pauses; the world is weird enough right now that she cannot dismiss lycanthropy as impossible. Something ripped the resort asunder. She cannot imagine a machine or natural disaster that could affect such destruction (snownado?), so she considers the supernatural.

"No," she decides, and steps forward.

It is a young man in a UCLA sweatshirt, his skin as gray as hoar-frost, sweating in spite of subzero temperatures, flip-flopping in the snow. His left arm flaps like a sleeve without a limb inside. At first, she thinks his arm might have been amputated, gone with the rest of the resort. But the sleeve looks heavy, and Xueman understands. He has dislocated his shoulder.

She kneels next to him as he lets out another howl, an animalistic sound more canine than coed. He is foaming at the mouth like a rabid beast. *The only thing that separates us from the animals is our capability for utter destruction,* Xueman thinks, recalling one of her professors' less po-etic assessments of humankind.

"I'm a doctor," Xueman tells the young man, trying to steady him as he kicks and screams.

He is not forming words. The pain has made him feral. She has seen many reactions to trauma from steely calm to chaotic histrionics. This lad's state is near the hysterical end of the scale. He obviously has not endured any great pain previously in his life. Like losing a husband. Like standing on the verge of losing a daughter.

Aspen.

Xueman looks around into the white. She almost gets up and leaves the young man behind. Aspen is out there. Somewhere. But she is a doctor, and this kid needs her.

Damn it.

The howling coed is not going to be any help, so Xueman dispenses with bedside manner. The only beds around anyway are through the snow, tottering at the edge of rooms ripped asunder. She grabs the arm slapping the snow like a fish flopping about on the frozen tundra. She puts her small foot against the kid's thin chest and pulls straight out without giving the complainer any warning. He screams like a screen siren dying beautifully in a slasher flick, then it is over.

The pain should have lessened by a great degree when she popped the ball joint back into the socket. But the kid turns to her, eyes still crazy with pain.

"Isn't it better?" Xueman asks, hoping he can fight through the agony to tell her what else is wrong.

Then she realizes she is now mistaking fear for pain. He is terrified. And he is not looking at Xueman. He's looking over her shoulder. Into the white.

"Behind you," he says.

-6°

Trevin and Alex are trapped.

Half of their room has been ripped away. The only thing left is one bed (the bed where they sinned), a rolling chair missing its desk, and a nightstand that surely contained a Gideon's Bible. Trevin was never one for Christianity, his sexuality damning him for all eternity and such, but he thinks maybe he could use the Good Book right about now to ward off…whatever that was that tore through the hotel like the Devil himself.

The rest is gone: bathroom, the door to the hall, the hall itself, and any escape in that direction. The balcony behind them offers a four-story fall. The precipice before them is a whiteout abyss where they might plunge for an eternity. Whatever razed the resort may have gouged a trench a million miles deep. Trevin imagines falling for forever into a pit of darkness without a bottom. Maybe Satan himself was coming to reap Trev's rotten soul and take it down to Hell for the things he did last night. Maybe the Bible is right about his sins. It isn't that he lay with a man, but he did lay with the *wrong* man.

Trevin turns his back on the abyss and returns to the balcony. Ski gear protects against most of the stinging wind, tiny grains peppering exposed cheeks and the cold stabbing the small area of exposed flesh like a thousand tiny needles. He cannot fathom what happened. Better to put it behind him. Ignore it. Move forward.

"We have got to get out of here, Trev," Alex whimpers. "The rest of this building could collapse at any moment."

There is not much left standing. In the brief lulls of the incessant wind, Trevin spots another balcony to his left. Nothing on the right. But there is no way to get across to that next balcony. No way back, either. The only escape is to jump.

The blizzard obscures everything: left, right, up, down. White everywhere. The only variation is quick glimpses of the other balcony. Otherwise, there is no hint as to what lies behind or below. The look on Alex's face confirms Trevin's own worries. Whatever smashed the structure the first time could come out of the white again at any moment.

Even if the event that crashed the resort was some natural phenomenon like a winter twister or a massive meteor shower or some new Russian satellite weapon that shot lasers from outer space and was just a one-time ordeal, they could not wait long up here in the stratosphere. The roof is gone, and it is like standing atop a mountain in a snowstorm. The temperature is dropping. The wind is wicked. The elements will claim them even if there is not a repeat occurrence of the previous disaster, something coming around again to finish the job it started. Without shelter, even with insulated ski gear, they will eventually freeze to death. Already, the snow is starting to layer on the carpet and pile along the single wall left standing. Trevin stares back at the frosted patio door, still intact, the most useless thing he has ever seen.

"We have to jump."

"Are you nuts?" Alex whines like a toddler that wants it to be Christmas when it is only August and expects you to do something about it. "We're four stories up! We'll break both legs if we jump. Or snap our necks."

"You just said we can't wait here," Trevin says.

"That doesn't mean I want to jump off a cliff, dude!"

"Is there a ladder around here that I haven't seen?"

"That doesn't mean we throw ourselves off the fourth floor," Alex argues. "Shit, Trev, you trying to kill yourself or something?"

Death is better than Trevin deserves right now. Death is the easy way out of the mess he has made. He cheated on David and the world cracked in half. Something out there is making sure he is punished for his sins.

"Can't we tie some sheets together and make a rope or something to climb down on?" Alex asks.

The sheets that they sinned under last night become the instruments of their salvation? Such ironic poetry only works in cheap fiction.

"This isn't a prison break movie, Alex. This is Butch Cassidy and the Sundance Kid."

"And you're supposed to be Butch?" Alex titters, nerves making his voice sound like he sucked helium. "Give me a break. More like a Bitch."

"It's a classic western, asshole. They jump into a river below them."

"A river would be frozen solid, Trev. So that plan is fucking stup—"

In the white, the bass sounds again. *Boom.*

Trevin jumps.

Into the white.

It is just a second, but it feels like forever. He used to always leap into the unknown, damn the consequences, deal with his choices the next day. But then there was David. Trevin settled down. He made better decisions. And wasn't there comfort in that? A steadiness? It eliminated that fearsome unknown that always lurked in his near future.

Then Trevin erased it all with one night.

He was so afraid of tomorrow that he made a mistake. Now today is scarier than any wedding because he is going to lose David. Now tomorrow is no longer a certainty, Armageddon arrived to wipe the world away, something terrible terrorizing the world. Trevin brought it here. Trevin and Alex and the sins of last night. They erased the future and doomed the present. Damn them.

Trevin hits bottom with an "Oof!" There is a snowdrift below the balcony some six feet high and enough to cushion the blow. His legs are stuck for a moment while he wiggles his way out, then he crawls down the small slope. He finds a shallow between the dunes of snow and steps away from the pile. From the white, he hears Alex shouting, sounding like he is a million miles away. The wind and snow serve to nearly erase his words.

Trevin considers leaving him behind. He wants to find David. He has to make sure his fiancé is still alive. Safe. He could run out into the white and leave Alex on the balcony, sure that Trevin is dead and unwilling to jump himself. Alex would stand up there until he died from exposure or whatever made the first pass through the resort comes back for the rest. Then David would never know that Trevin cheated. The future could be different.

"Jump," Trevin calls up. "Jump!"

He waits. Nothing. He shouts again. Nothing. Again. Somewhere in the white, the thunder rolls once more. Trevin stops shouting. He cannot tell if the sound is a mile away or just across the courtyard. The thing that makes that sound and wrecked the resort could be right in the white. Close.

He stares as the alabaster swirls and swishes. White on white on white on white. Forever.

The snow makes shapes, Trevin's heart thudding like its own thunder in his chest. Something there? Then gone again. Something else? Then nothing. Movement? Constant shifting. Shadows might be a form or formed from snow shadow. The blizzard obscures. Trevin could be surrounded by danger, or there might be nothing in every direction.

Then something is right behind him.

His voice catches, like a chunk of hot dog lodged in his esophagus. His bladder lets go, warmth running down his legs and trickling into his boots. The sound is a muffled thump, a small version of the reverberating boom that recurred every few minutes. It is smaller, but it is right beside him. Close enough to attack.

It reaches out from the white and grabs Trevin by the coat.

"I twisted my goddamn ankle when I hit the snowbank," Alex whines.

Fucking Alex.

And because there is no imminent danger to fend off, no doomed future to fight, no monster to scratch and kick and hit, Trevin balls his right hand into a fist and hits Alex Dove as hard as he can, knocking the bastard unconscious.

-7°

Black.

Completely black.

Zack is still alive. For someone intent on ending his life just an hour ago, he certainly did not just let the end engulf him when the roof of the resort caved in. He'd thrown himself into the cast iron cauldron as all matter of fuck came down on his head. The sound was like the end of the world. It lasted for just a moment, a crushing, crashing cacophony, and then just silence. Complete quiet.

And then the black.

He'd lost his phone when he jumped into the ancient, empty boiler. It is somewhere outside the door, now barricaded by debris. He waves his hand (still gripping the pistol) in front of his face for the fiftieth time, but his eyes cannot adjust to this dark. The pitch is absolute. He has never known such darkness.

He has never felt so alone.

Just Zack and the gun.

An hour ago, he was ready to blow his own brains out. Now he is trapped under a building that seems to have been demolished right on top of him, and he feels like a trapped rabbit that would gnaw off its own paw just to escape. He feels around for the doorway to the boiler, but there is just concrete and rebar and steel beams blocking the way. Not a single ray of light filters through. There is no escape.

He is going to die down here. A slow and horrible death. "I'll starve," he had said aloud, and the echo that had resounded in the vast vat gave him chills. He did not say anything aloud again. *No*, he realized, *I will die of thirst before I starve.* That was an hour ago. Now, a chill starts to set in against the wall of the cast iron container. Zack has craved contact with the side of the boiler as some anchor against the amorphous dark, but the cold is worse than being alone. He pushes himself away. *The cold will get me before the thirst.*

The bullet could end it before hunger, thirst, or cold claimed him.

Somewhere beyond the cast iron walls of the boiler, a bass sound makes the metal vibrate beneath the balls of Zack's feet. The gun could solve his problem before he was killed off by frost, lack of food, the absence of water…or whatever made that sound.

Now that he should, he couldn't. The gun in his hand seems too heavy, but he is too afraid to put it aside, scared he won't be able to find it again. When it gets bad enough, he might get brave enough to use it. And he is too nervous to tuck it in his waistband, worried he has the safety backward and he turned it off when he thought he was putting it on. Zack did not want to accidentally shoot his dick off in an abandoned boiler and slowly bleed to death.

Zack wants out.

He feels his way to the doorway again, taking more time to survey the blockage. A small piece of rebar pulls loose, giving him momentary hope. Nothing else even wiggles. With probing fingers, he explores a gap between the cast iron side of the doorway and a chunk of concrete near the basement floor. Zack wedges the rod of rebar into the crevasse. After placing the gun under the sole of his shoe, he grabs the bar with both hands. The Gurp throws his considerable weight against the rod, leaning and pushing, until a block the size of a shoebox pops loose and lands with a *thud.* Zack reaches into the small hole created by the loosened chunk.

He flinches back. Something bit his hand! He imagines small alien parasites that arrived on spaceships that destroyed the resort coming to exterminate the last of humanity. He grabs for the gun, ready to blow any extraterrestrials off the face of his world.

He pauses.

His finger is bleeding, but it is not a bite. It is a cut. Glass. He reaches in again, more carefully.

"My phone," he exclaims, wincing as his voice bounces around the room.

The screen is shattered, but the home button is intact and activates the light. He squints against the sudden brightness. The shattered screen only works in an indecipherable kaleidoscope, but Zack knows damn well what the last thing he had up on his screen. He could not change the page or activate the flashlight, so the half-lit screen, colored maudlin blues and deep, dark grays, is all he has to see by. Compared to complete darkness, it is like a torch fending off the night.

The feeble glow only illuminates a foot in front of his face. Beyond, it is just shadows blending with black. Zack surveys the blockage in the access door more thoroughly. The rest of the debris is big and jammed like tangled twigs in a beaver dam. The faint light catches a cloud of his breath. Even if he could manage to dislodge some of the detritus, it would take longer than he had. The temperature is dropping precipitously. There is a way out, there is *always* a way out, but leaving the same way he got in is not an option. With the light, he can look to see if there is another exit.

The top of his screen remains the only area not rendered into jumbled pixels. The battery symbol shows he is at sixty-three percent. At least something is going right. Sixty-three percent should give him ample time to survey the entire interior of the boiler.

Zack is paralyzed.

First, he had been scared of life. Then he was scared to die. He was scared of the interior of the boiler. Now he is scared of whatever is on the other side of the cast iron shell. He was terrified of the dark. Now he is so afraid of what he might see that he cannot take a single step. He is even too frightened to turn off the light to save battery. He stays immobile for long minutes, watching the number on his battery reserves tick down from sixty-three to sixty-two to sixty-one. And the imaginary thermometer in his mind also drops, -5° to -6° to -7°. And the Gurp doesn't move. He is too damned scared.

And then he hears digging.

At first, he thinks it might be a rescue squad, but the mass of material giving a dull squeal and thrumming through the metal walls of the container is too big for men digging their way in. It would take a bulldozer and a backhoe, and there is no such construction equipment on the mountain in the middle of winter. Besides, no one knew Zack even came down here. No *person* knew.

Whatever makes that noise is something else. It sounds like a dog digging up a bone that's buried too deep. Maybe Zack is the last person alive on the whole mountain? Maybe he is a last Gurppy dessert for hungry aliens. Whatever is out there is big enough to raze the resort, so it could certainly mine the earth for one last morsel.

"Fuck." Zack exhales, too low to cause any echo, just enough to cause a brief puff of white that glints momentarily in the light of his phone before it dissipates.

Zack steps away from the access door. He starts moving clockwise around the boiler as the digging continues outside the iron wall. Steel screeches against concrete somewhere out there.

More metal, more metal, more metal. He is disconcerted about the frost building up on the inside surface of the tank, but he wonders if he will not live long enough to freeze to death anyway. Zack suspects the thing that is digging for him wants a warm meal.

Zack comes upon an access pipe on the other side of the tank. When the boiler was working, it carried a stream of hot water to a series of other pipes throughout the hotel. Zack considers how likely it is that the larger pipe had some exit along the length, or if it merely diverts into successively smaller branches, reducing until it is no bigger than the plumbing under his kitchen sink. Even this tube is hardly large enough for Zack to fit his oversized ass. If the diameter reduced at all, he would be stuck along a length of cast iron barely as big across as a coffin.

Zack shudders.

"Shit," he hisses, and a sibilant echo repeats down the length of the pipe.

The digging has stopped. For now. It will start again if Zack remains in the cauldron. He is sure of it.

He takes a deep breath.

Wedging in, his back scrapes the top when he lifts his knee to creep forward. His wide backside barely clears the opening of the outlet. He still has his phone in one hand, and the gun is in the other. One deep breath. Then he starts going forward.

-8°

Roman Carver has never set foot on the property operated by the Enchanted Point Ski Resort, just a half mile from the cabin he had called home these last twenty years. Now it appears he is too late to ever have the chance. He checks the compass on his wrist, the glass frosty. The needles are visible through a thin layer of ice. This is the place. Forty paces from the edge of the woods. He had been that close hundreds of times. Close enough. The northeast wing should have been a hundred feet from the dying spruce. So he paced out a hundred feet, only to find more snow.

Roman digs through a snowbank. Beneath the layer of white is travertine tile, imported from overseas.

Probably the lobby.

He pauses for a moment, hunkered down to look at the floor, head cocked so his ear is in the wind. Even with all his experience, the wind erases direction and makes sound seem to come from anywhere. Muffled and meandering, a noise could be in the east and far away or from the north and close enough to strike.

Then comes the sound he is waiting for. Thunder.

Roman is comforted by the baritone boom that sounds off occasionally. He's sure he is dealing with a predator. And no predator clever enough to stalk human prey announces itself when it is close enough to strike. The thing in the white does not intend an impending attack. As soon as Roman hears the thunderous clap, he moves. The ominous sound does not give him pause; it's the silence that makes him nervous.

He makes his way west, toward the south wing. There is no sign of the four-story structure that had already stood here for decades before Roman had even arrived on Bailey's Peak. What could sweep away an entire resort in a matter of moments? What massive monster made that sound off somewhere in the white? What the hell happened here?

He finds the edge of the former structure. The foundation forms an unnatural line in the snow, a bank more or less straight as it stretches and disappears into the white. The mountain slopes downward in this direction, and Roman steps over the edge of the foundation.

And stops.

The white gives and takes, wiping away the distance, then giving a peek again. There was an old codger who had passed by Roman's cabin a few years back with his son. The old man had gone snow blind, lost up on the peak during a sunny winter day, and now fumbled after his kid, who had been smart enough to wear tinted goggles. Roman had sent them on down Bailey's Peak in the direction of Zukunft Falls, where they could find medical attention. But there are other kinds of snowblind. The shifting effects of the blowing snow made things appear and disappear, like shapes in the clouds made from one's imagination.

Shadows in the white suggest something massive. Roman remains still, perhaps as hidden by the blowing blizzard as the object he is looking at. Is it the thing that made the sound? The monster that had razed the resort? Or something else?

Something else.

He gauges whether the behemoth changed position or if it is just the effect of the blowing snow. He marks the edges against a backdrop as amorphous as a bank of fog. After long minutes of staring at the shape, Roman decides it has remained as still as he has. He steps forward.

He has seen snowbanks as high as trees, the tops making the tips of thirty-foot firs look like little potted plants someone might keep on their window sill. After a hell of a storm six years ago, he had to dig himself out of a window in his cabin, and when he walked around to the front of his home, he found a sloping bank had swept up and over his roof, making the cabin a part of the landscape. Up the mountain, Roman once observed an incline that ended with a forty-foot drop-off, and it was not until the next spring that he realized nothing but snow had made up the white hill.

But this is something else.

It towers twenty feet and stretches along until it disappears in each direction. The snow already covers a lot of it, filling cracks and obscuring edges. It's a mountain of debris, the demolished remains of the resort, piled relatively neatly along a ridge that looks more like a wall than individual mounds. Whatever the shape, it looks like it has *purpose*.

Somewhere, another boom. He feels safe. For now.

"Help," comes a soft whisper behind him, although the snow muffles the sound; it might have been a scream.

Roman turns. Ten feet away, half in focus through the driven snow, stands a young woman huddled inside a pink blanket. The cover is barely big enough to cover her torso. She wears mismatched boots, one white and furry, the other black and shiny. Bare knees show below the cuff of the blanket and above the edge of the boots, skin already worrisomely white. The knees are knocking together.

Roman rushes forward as the young woman swoons, topples. He catches her before her head hits the ground. Her eyes are glazed, and she mumbles deliriously as the early stages of hypothermia set in.

"Mmmma?" she slurs.

Roman pulls off his bearskin coat and wraps the young woman in it. She is not shivering. Not good. The wind bites Roman, and he ignores the fangs. He has his own fur, a thick coat of hair left long enough to fend off the long winters.

He checks the compass and sets a course for the south wing. He plunges into the white without hesitation, carrying the bundle in his arms as easily as a mother with a swaddled babe. The south wing is a hundred yards from the place where he found the young woman, but he does not see any more survivors along the way. Nor victims covered under sheets of snow.

The predator is impressively efficient. Roman uses every part of his kills: he uses blood and ground bones for fertilizer, antlers for weapons and tools such as the dagger tucked in his belt, hides for clothes and blankets, feathers for down pillows and his mattress, and everything else for food. This predator has left no offal behind after the attack.

And then there is the barrier of debris he saw around the partial perimeter of the resort. Like the makings of a trap.

The skeleton of the hotel appears within the white, taking vague shape and resolving by degrees as Roman approaches. It has been torn asunder, the rubble cleared cleanly away, just a shell open to the elements, the remaining rooms exposed like a full-sized architectural model. In another life, Roman was in charge of departments that made scale versions that looked like these: cutaway representations of proposed designs that were lifelike down to every last detail.

Roman stands still. The wind is just a puff of air on the leeward side. Dozens of open alcoves are visible, snow gathering inside fancy hotel rooms because they are all missing walls. But awe could too easily hypnotize someone, so he shakes it off. Roman needs to keep his wits about him. His eyes sweep the scene, and past the edge of the shelter belt through the thick wall of white he sees tracks half-buried in a stairwell. Survivors. They had trekked down the flight of stairs and gathered at the bottom. Roman considers the direction of the prints. They lead north, into the small village of Zukunft Falls, which consists of homes and businesses that support the resort. Roman plunges back into the blizzard, the wind a shriek given substance. The trail sometimes disappears, buried under drifts of snow or obliterated by the wind, but he is as good a tracker as anyone living in these mountains and finds the trail again every time.

He stops. The young woman in his arms is pressed against his chest, protected inside his furs from the furious winds. It is white all around. The tracks continue, but it has been long minutes since he last heard the unnatural thunder. That means the predator could be anywhere. If it is quiet, that might mean the hunter is hunting. It might be hunting Roman. He crouches, the cold numbing without the essential protection of his fur coat. He cannot survive much longer against the elements, and he will not do the woman any favors by dying before he gets her to shelter. Yet whatever is attacking also consumes its prey entirely, and he is loathe to become fertilizer and food for something else. And this young woman's mother would never know that her daughter had come looking for her.

He stares into the white as if he can sort flake from flake and see beyond. But past snow is more snow. White on white. His imminent death might snatch him from the alabaster curtain at any moment. His time could come in the next blink of an eye, before his next breath. Roman cannot see. He can't see what is coming next.

Then the baritone clangor comes. Somewhere else. The predator either found other prey and sounds rejoice, or the thunderous boom is the effect of further destruction. Maybe it is a mating call. Whatever it is, it is a sign that Roman is safe. For now.

He plunges ahead, into the white.

-9°

Rhonda settles Esther on a small cot in the corner. She opens a bottle of water and hands it to the old woman. Esther shakes, the lip of the bottle on a trajectory to miss her mouth until Rhonda reaches out and gently corrects the direction. She takes a sip, then clutches the plastic container like it is a warm cup of tea. Esther's gaze scans the room as if she is looking for something, but she doesn't appear to recall just what it is.

She is looking for Clarice. Rhonda remembers.

"Why don't you wait here, Esther," Rhonda says.

Esther glances up and for a moment seems poised to ask just why the hell a stranger is asking her to do anything. Instead, the old woman nods. Rhonda is not sure how far along the disease is, or if she suffers Alzheimer's or Parkinson's or early stages of dementia, but Esther has already started adjusting. Acting that everything is alright. The woman is adept enough to still stick to the societal script. If someone knows your name, then you probably ought to know them back. So Esther pretends.

They had followed the majority down to a small village set north of the razed resort. A smaller group had splintered off from the crowd and ventured toward the northeast wing of the hotel, where one resort employee swore there was an avalanche shelter. Rhonda equated an "avalanche shelter" to a bomb shelter or a tornado shelter. She pictured a small underground room with concrete walls and limited provisions. Such a shelter could not be designed to hold more than a half dozen survivors, and five times that many had gone off to find the avalanche shelter. Rhonda would rather take her chances in the wide, white open before being packed like canned sardines.

She did not know what was happening yet, so she remained unwilling to be cramped inside a ten-by-ten vault with thirty other people. Besides, something that smashed a four-story structure could just as easily dig out an underground vault.

The rest of the survivors numbered almost a hundred. They ventured down the slope to the village en masse, keeping children and elderly to the inside of the crowd to protect them from the worst of the wind and cold. Like a herd of confused cattle. Rhonda remembered registering the group of homes and businesses in her peripheral vision as she arrived in Zukunft Falls, the taxi taking her along a road to the resort that went right through town. Quaint ranch style homes built of life-sized Lincoln Logs. A small grocery store, a gas station, a couple of churches, three bars. An elementary school at the edge of town that is big enough to hold all of them.

As the tourists that made up the majority of the herd followed the locals who worked at the resort through town, Rhonda worried that whatever razed the resort had already destroyed the school. The frigid wind cut through her winter coat, and the gray scarf she got from Howard only minimized the effect of the cold. She worried about Esther, trudging along through drifts as high as, and sometimes higher than, their knees. The collective body heat from the crowd of a hundred was all that sustained them. But they needed shelter. Someplace warm. Sooner rather than later. What if the school was also in ruins?

The school was still standing. The handyman Rhonda recognized from the resort also acted as the custodian at the school. He had a key and let them all inside the back door to the gymnasium. There were already hundreds of resort refugees inside the school, displaced tourists and homeless locals who worked and lived at Enchanted Point. Huddled masses sat on bleachers, and wretched survivors curled alone in corners, so many softly crying. When the unnatural thunder occasionally sounded, everyone hushed, as if silence could protect them.

Now, Rhonda wanders around the gymnasium looking for Clarice Otter. The only lights are emergency bulbs running off the generator, giving off a dull red glow that makes everyone look vaguely demonic. Fitting for a situation that seemed like Hell on earth. If Hell had frozen over. About four hundred people have gathered in the gym, with more arriving every few minutes. The custodian chained the six sets of exit doors around the room and stands sentry near the one that leads outside. Rhonda wonders what the chains are meant to keep out; whatever wreaked havoc on the resort had to be too big to fit through the doors, and mere chains would not suffice in keeping it out even if it did come knocking.

Still, every time someone rattled the doors, the custodian unlocked the chains and opened up. The latest arrival came ten minutes ago, a burly black man who looked more savage than civilized, carrying a young Asian woman who looked frozen to death when he unwrapped her from a bearskin coat. Several tourists gathered about, gawking as much as helping. The black man looked like he would rather be outside taking his chances with whatever stalked them in the white rather than be stuck inside with all these strangers.

The chains rattle as Rhonda passes the door leading outside and she about has a heart attack. *You're not too old for that to happen,* her sinister self reminds her. The custodian is looking over the young Asian woman, who seems to be stirring. He looks up as the chains jangle, pulling the key off the retractable device on his belt as he hustles over.

Rhonda waits to see who arrives. Clarice is not amongst the survivors already inside the gym, so Rhonda needs to take a full inventory of any newcomers. The latest arrival is a woman entering solo, but much too young to be Esther's traveling companion. She unzips a coat stiff with cold, showing a waitress uniform underneath and a name tag that says "Eva."

Tears are frozen in beads on freckled cheeks, curious gems that sparkle pink when they catch the scarlet glow of the emergency lights. Eva sobs uncontrollably, stumbling forward on legs that seem stiff as icicles.

"Marty with you?" the custodian asks, holding the door open a few inches, searching the white behind her.

She shakes her head, unable to make any other sound than a wounded mewling.

"Anyone else?" he asks over the whining wind. Snow dashes in the crack of the door, flakes fluttering in the faint red light before disappearing in a wink in the relative warmth.

She shakes her head again.

Eva collapses in a heap on the slat-board floor of the gymnasium as the custodian locks the chain again. Another local approaches. He is a middle-aged man with no hair.

"Eva? What happened?"

"Marty," she manages to moan, before the sound descends into sobs.

"Wasn't Marty with the party that went on up to the avalanche shelter?" the bald local asks.

Eva nods. "Landlines still work. He called me at the diner. From the shelter. He said it was safe. He was there with Bob Kline, Mary Ashland, Kerry Chu. They were all calling their loved ones to the shelter to join them. They planned on packing us in like clowns in a car. So I headed on up."

She breaks down again. Rhonda steps between the two men and puts a hand on Eva's shoulder, patting her. Eva stands and pulls Rhonda into a big hug, sobbing against the stranger's shoulder. Rhonda does not know what to say to this woman she has never met, so she just hugs her.

Finally, Eva pulls away, running the back of her sleeve across her mess of a face. She looks Rhonda in the eye and nods. Then she turns to the bald man and the custodian. "I got there too late. Or late enough, maybe some would say. Allan Ashland got there just before me. The wind died long enough for the white to reveal him standing at the entrance to the shelter. Then a gust came up, just a split-second whoosh of white, and then he was gone. Maybe he got inside awful quick, I thought. I took another step closer. Then the earth itself overturned. Like a backhoe the size of the fucking diner scooping up snow and soil, it lifted up and away, into the white."

"What was it?" the bald man interrupts.

Eva shrugs. "I couldn't see a damn thing through the snow. But it was big. Bigger than anything. Then it scooped again. The fucking thing was digging for the avalanche shelter. I mean, that shelter is ten feet underground, but the thing *knew* it was there. Scoop, scoop, scoop. Deeper and deeper. I started to step back, afraid it would see me. Afraid it would get me like it got Allan. The white swallowed up the scene, but I could still hear the muffled sounds of digging, digging, digging. Then worse. Screeching metal and screaming. People screaming."

Eva buries her face in Rhonda's shoulder. "One of them screaming was Marty."

Rhonda rubs the middle of Eva's back. What the hell kind of monster is out there? She feels like breaking down herself. Then she sees the black man who brought in the frozen young woman just at the edge of shadows. He stands alone, listening. And there is something in his uncivilized eyes. Understanding. And fear.

-10°

David sees shadows off to his right and cannot be sure if it is a nearby building or whatever he saw in the white. Sitting in the street would mean death due to exposure, so he moves forward. He manages to drag the unconscious doctor through the snow toward the shadow as it settles into a rare section of shelter still standing along the site of the former resort. It is a shed that houses a row of snow blowers along one wall and shovels hanging perfectly straight on frosted metal hooks above them. Once upon a time, these would be the tools needed as soon as the snow stopped. Now, the caretakers of the Enchanted Point Ski Resort will need something a hell of a lot bigger than this meek fleet of arctic cats to clear the mess out there in the white.

The room smells like oil and reminds David of back home in Kearney, at his Dad's repair shop where he had once worked, cleaning up the place every day after school. His Dad had always tried to teach him about vehicles and pass on his infinite knowledge of mechanics, but David had always been thinking about poetry and dreaming too much about the way rhymes might fit together to ever learn anything about engines. He was lucky to get out of Nebraska remembering how to switch his own oil and swap out a tire. Then he found out no one in California changed their own oil or tires. No one in L.A. changed at all.

Except Trevin. Trev had been a playboy when David first met him at a club that seemed more Oz than America. Trev had started out telling stories of mythic conquests like he thought himself some modern-day Odysseus enduring trials that usually occurred between the sheets. That first night, Trev told him that love is just a fairy tale, and there were no princes or happily ever afters. That had been four-and-a-half years ago.

Six months ago, Trevin had proposed. And David had said yes.

This was supposed to have been their bachelor party. Now David does not know if his fiancé is even still alive. The only person he knows isn't dead is the doctor lying unconscious in front of a propane heater that he had turned on to low. These machines freeze up when the temperatures get too cold, so the heater is here to keep them warm enough to start. This inherent nature of mechanical things might end up saving his life. Wouldn't his dad think that's the darnedest thing?

It's getting colder outside, dropping to dangerous degrees. If they had still been exposed to the elements, they would have lasted only scant minutes before frostbite set in, or hypothermia affected them. Visibility is down to being measured in inches. He would not survive dragging the doc's dead weight through the blizzard.

The Asian woman stirs, then slowly sits up, blinking away the confusion. She looks at David like he is a stranger, then she remembers and she exhales. She moans as she touches her head.

"You fainted," David informs her. "Luckily, the snow cushioned the fall."

"Where are we?" the doctor asks.

"A shed," David says. "It was close enough that I could drag you. Even with my shoulder." He winces at the mention of it.

"Aspen," she recites, like a motivation for motion. She tries to stand, swoons, almost pitches forward into the propane flames before plopping back on her butt.

"Whoa, Doc," David warns. He reaches out with his good arm and puts his hand on her shoulder. "Easy does it."

"I have to find my daughter," the doctor says.

"You saw what's out there."

The doctor pauses. Frowns. Winces. "Did I? I don't really know what the hell I saw."

"You saw enough to faint dead away. You could have killed us both, keeling over instead of running!"

"I saved your ass, kid. It was probably your incessant screaming that drew it near in the first place."

"You saved me. I saved you. Even Steven."

"What did you see? All I could make out was a…" The doctor trails off and shudders.

"Shadow," David whispers. "Like a fucking 747 passing behind a cloud."

"What do you think it was?"

David shrugs. "It was the end of the world as we know it."

"I thought I was dead."

"Probably closer than we'll ever know. After you fainted, it just disappeared. I could hear it, maybe near, maybe far. The wind and snow play tricks, you know. But it was digging. I could feel the ground under me *hum*, like a train was passing nearby. I think—" David pauses. Doc is looking for her daughter. She doesn't need to hear the next part. Trevin is missing, too. David doesn't need to think about the next part. "I heard people screaming."

"It followed the food. More plentiful prey."

David does not answer that.

Doc lights up a cigarette without asking David if he minds her polluting the constricted interior of the small shed. Politeness has taken a back seat.

"Do you really need to do that?" David sneers.

"I definitely do," Doc answers, puffing the stick down to nothing. When she finishes, she stubs the butt on her heel and places it in a trash can under a workbench.

"You have loved ones out there?" Doc asks.

David nods.

"Then we can't stay here."

"Well, we can at least look for some kind of weapon," David says. "This is a tool shed. There must be something we can use to defend ourselves."

"Whatever that was, it tore through a four-story building like a toddler through a Lego city. You think a hedge trimmer and a leaf blower are going to do anything?"

"It'll make me feel better," David says with grit. "I bet a hornet dies with a smirk on its face if it gets a good sting in before being swatted into oblivion. I might not stand a chance in hell against whatever that thing is out there, but I am going to sting that motherfucker like a bee before I go splat."

Doc grins. "Gumption."

"I might scream like a girl, but I fight like a lioness," David declares, swinging his fists around like the big cat from *Wizard of Oz*. David winces and rubs his wounded shoulder.

"Alright," the doctor says. She gets to her feet and starts looking around the shed, shadows dancing from the flames. "Rakes. Shovels. I have shears."

"I am thinking more flamethrower."

"Chainsaw?"

"With my bum shoulder, that will have to be all you, Doc. You know how to run one?"

"My husband showed me. A long time ago."

"You still remember?"

"I still remember," she says.

David finds a pick for chipping away the shells of ice after a storm coats the resort. He knows an ice pick, and he knows chainsaws, and he knows snow. David had spent a lifetime in Nebraska before he ran away to Cali. Nebraska had been awful, and the winters had been awfully cold for being hell. Cold, but not *this* cold. David shivers. The thermometer on the outside of the shed when he dragged Doc inside was well below the zero mark.

"I'll take this," he says, jabbing the point at the fire. He likes that it's a stinger. Like a killer bee.

Doc approaches with a roll of duct tape. "First, we immobilize that shoulder. It pops out, and you'll be screaming all over again." She wraps him up like a Christmas gift, winding the roll around his arm again and again. "Now your ice pick. You're never going to hang on to that with those mittens, and your fingers will freeze and fall off without them." David nods. Doc attaches the handle of the ice pick to his forearm with the duct tape, the point sticking out over his hand so that when he bends at the wrist, it protrudes for easy impalement.

David walks to the door. He looks back. She carries a chainsaw and a grimace. "Gumption," he says.

"Gumption," she agrees.

And they step out into the white.

-11°

Trevin thought about leaving Alex in the snow. He probably would have never come to, sleep taking him away and waking never arriving, the white stealing his life while he was unconscious. It might have been a mercy. While he lay limp and lifeless in the bank of snow, the unnerving thunderclap sounded somewhere in the storm again. Whatever had made that noise, it would be far better to just close your eyes and dream away than face whatever fate awaits the victims of the thing in the white.

Dead men tell no tales. His indiscretion with Alex would remain a secret. Trevin would find David, and they would get out of this place together. Mourn this tragedy and move on. Trevin would say nice things about Alex in the casket before him, then David would shed a tear because David is the crying kind at funerals. But then Alex would fade away, only occasionally revisited in Trevin's darker thoughts, in moments of guilt and lust.

In the end, he drags Alex to the remaining section of the south wing that's still standing, just four feet away from where Trevin decked Alex and yet still invisible except for the occasional lull in the wind. Trevin pulls Alex by sections of walls that have been ripped away, revealing cubicles of rooms, some furniture left in a few, a bed here and there, a television hanging on the wall in case mythic monsters in the white might want to watch some CNN. He finds a room that still has four walls and a roof and an open door, the inhabitants gone with whatever survivors lived through the initial attack.

The electricity is off. Inside, despite shelter from the wind, it is already dangerously cold. Trevin wraps Alex in blankets and props his deadweight ass against a wall. He sits on the bed and stares out the window for a while, the glass somehow defying the frost and giving a clear view to the whiteout beyond. Suddenly, he is sure that something is staring back. Trevin is frozen. He doesn't even breathe. Doesn't blink. Whatever is out there swept through the resort and razed most of the hotel in moments. If it wants Trevin dead, moving or breathing or blinking won't be what seal his fate.

He gets up, strides across the room, and pulls the drapes closed. If death is coming, he does not want to see its approach.

"What did you do that for?" Alex asks behind him, startling Trevin.

"I was tired of looking at the white," Trevin whispers.

"No," Alex whines, like a kid who had a toy taken away. "Why did you hit me?"

"Because someone needed to hit you, and I was the only one around."

Alex sulks. Trevin glares at the drapes. Silence stretches between them. Alex cannot handle silence.

"Are we going to stay here?" Alex asks.

"I need to find David," Trevin says.

"I don't want to go out there. We'll freeze."

"We will freeze if we stay here."

"Then we run," Alex says. "Find a truck or a Jeep or one of those arctic cats and head down the mountain."

"Not without David."

"Fuck David," Alex sneers. "Why do you want to find him for anyway? To break his heart? Just so you can die together? Because whatever it is out there wants to kill us all."

"We don't have to tell him today. Let's live to see tomorrow before we worry too much about it."

Tomorrow. He had been afraid of it ever since they became engaged. Tomorrow was the shadow that stalked you in the alleyway, the darkness that dangerously dimmed the breezeway between your backdoor and the garage, the shade in the corner of your bedroom at three in the morning that you were *almost* sure did not just move. It was always just right over there and scary as hell. But now, tomorrow is the thing that Trevin wants more than anything. Yet it seems further away than ever.

"It's over, Trev. You want it to be over. So let it go. Leave him alone."

"I still love him, Alex," Trevin snaps. "I can't just turn my back and leave him here! I need to know what happened to him. Is he safe? Is he dead? Does he need me? Is he out there looking for me?"

"I don't know if there is anyone out there," Alex grumbles.

Then someone pounds on the door. Trevin is standing by the door and jumps. Alex squeaks like a frightened mouse. Trevin scowls at the man who had been his lover short hours ago. He peers out the peephole. Outside the door is a hallway that looks like a thousand other hotels across America, just with wisps of snow whipping by on blustery winds and fingers of white drawn against the walls on either side of the corridor. Standing in the interior snowstorm is a fat kid with snotcicles hanging from each nostril and enough frost in his mangy eyebrows to wring out and make a snow cone.

Trevin opens the door, and the kid stumbles in. He is no more than eighteen and blubbering like he is four. Something about his momma. He flaps his arms like an excited chicken although he looks more like a flustered piglet. Tears stand frozen, like crystals, in the corners of his eyes. Trevin is trapped with a bunch of pansy-asses.

Trevin slaps the kid across the face, the fat cheek absorbing the blow like the big backside of a cuddly bear at the clubs Trevin used to attend every Saturday night. Trevin has only punched one person in his entire life and that was Alex about an hour ago, but he has slapped the shit out of many a bitch in his day.

"Quit your blubbering or you can take your chances with what-ever is out there," Trevin says. "We aren't going to get anywhere while you're sniffling and bawling like a goddamn baby."

The kid inhales louder than anything this side of the mysterious thunder that cracks the world every so often. His mouth quivers like Jell-o in a Cali quake, but he finally manages to form a string of words that doesn't sound like Farsi. "What happened?" he asks.

"Monsters, kid," Trevin says. "They're real after all. If your mama told you different, then she's a lying whore."

The kid squeezes his eyes shut. "She's probably dead."

"Jesus, Trev. He's just scared. Take it easy, for Chrissakes."

"This isn't *easy*, Alex. And it isn't getting any easier. She probably *is* dead. And maybe so is David."

Silence descends upon the room. No one has anything more to say about that. In the absence of conversation, the temperature gets their attention.

"It's cold in here," the kid comments. He wears a thick sweater, but no gloves, no hat, no coat. How did he survive even two minutes out there?

Cold.

Trevin looks at the drapes concealing the world beyond the small room. There are shadows in the corners and darkness in the distance, but that doesn't seem so scary anymore. The truly terrifying things exist in the white. They roam in the wide open, stalking their prey.

It is cold everywhere.

"We need to go," Trevin says. "We'll make our way down the slope. Look for vehicles. Pick up any survivors along the way. Maybe there is strength in numbers."

Maybe multiple targets increase the odds that the thing out there in the white will grab someone else other than Trevin. This fat guy is twice his size, and if the thing in the snow eats its prey, the dude has to look a lot more appetizing than Trevin.

"What's your name, dude?"

"Zack."

"Well, Zack, stick close," Trevin says, thinking Zack is the newest appetizer on the menu. "We're getting out of this town."

-12°

Esther watches the people come and go and wonders if she should know any of them. Her memory is slippery nowadays. It is worse when she is nervous or under stress. Armageddon has accelerated all of her symptoms. She came to this resort with Clarice to relax and arrest the progression of degeneration, but then the end of the world occurred. Now she does not recall really what happened, who helped her escape, and which one of the hundred strangers she might know by name.

She wants to remember the woman who brought her here. She knows it was a woman because she could remember men better than women for some reason. Especially handsome men. But the ladies slipped away like milk through a cheesecloth. Sometimes a curd would remain. Usually, the cream drained away, leaving her with nothing.

"Do I know you?" Esther asks the woman nearest where she stood in the high school gymnasium. The woman wears yoga pants and a sweatshirt advertising a Pilates class, though she looks neither in shape for yoga nor interested in exercise. It is a question Esther often asks lately. She should have been asking, "Am I supposed to know you?"

The woman gives her a strange, sour look, like Esther had soiled her pants instead of having asked a simple question. Esther smiles and pretends everything is okay. She pretends a lot nowadays.

She remembers the old things. Like Clarice Otter. They were friends in grammar school and had stayed in touch over the years. When Esther's husband died and Clarice called to offer condolences, their old friendship reignited. Esther remembers Clarice better than just about anyone. The middle stuff is iffy. Sometimes she forgets a grand-child, or misremembers one of their names, or cannot recall if Quinn is a boy or a girl. She isn't sure if *Steel Magnolias* was a few years ago or a lot of years ago. She can picture with perfect clarity her wedding ceremony with Walt, but she cannot recount almost any detail of his funeral. Sometimes, she forgets that he is dead. Remembering again is hard. Some things would be nice if they stayed forgotten.

She has learned to fake things. When someone starts talking, Esther always talks to them as if she has known them for years because she might have. Sometimes Clarice would go on and on about something some politician had done or the goings on of a television show they supposedly watched, and Esther would nod along like she under-stood the context of every word. There are ways of answering questions that are not really answers at all, so no one can call you on your bull-shit. Little meaningless phrases like, "Wouldn't that be nice," and "Whatever will be will be."

"Tomorrow will be worse than today," her doctor had told her when he had diagnosed the Alzheimer's. "And the next day will be worse than that. And so on. Now, there will be exceptions, but most days will follow the rule. I am sorry, Missus Williams. Just keep trying to enjoy each day."

Esther remembers that. She can't quite recall who brought her to this high school gymnasium in a snowstorm, or even why they are all gathered in a school rather than a hotel, but she does remember some-one brought her here. *Someone.* What's-her-name. Esther scans the gym-nasium, but she doesn't see even one face she recognizes.

The world doesn't make sense anymore. Esther absentmindedly wrings her hands. She has always done that when she is anxious, and she is anxious all the time lately. Strangers look at her like she doesn't belong here, and everyone is a stranger. Gadgets glow in the gloom, making beeps and burps that she does not understand. Half the words mean something other than what she remembers them to mean: nets, clouds, text, trolls, tweets, sick. She does not know why she is here, where she is at, and what she is supposed to do. The world went white long before she came to the Montana mountains.

Esther wants to cry, but grown women do not cry in polite company. Looking around, a few grown women are weeping in the shadows, and several men are unashamedly sobbing. They look scared. Esther is scared, too, but she does not know what she is supposed to be scared of. If she starts bawling, someone will ask her why, and she can't very well answer with, "Wouldn't that be nice."

She wants to run, but something in the fog of remembrance warns against that, like an emergency light blinking red behind the veil of the blizzard. Esther stays put.

"Excuse me, should I know you?" Esther asks a woman nearby. The woman wears inappropriate yoga pants and a sweatshirt. Esther doesn't realize it is the same woman she asked before. The woman scowls.

"I know you, Esther."

It is a black woman who Esther doesn't remember, but she fakes it. "Of course," Esther answers, like they are old friends who go back to days in the nursery, although this woman is twenty years younger (and trying unsuccessfully to look more like half Esther's age).

"There are some people that want to go down the mountain. Get out of here. What do you think, Esther?"

If What's-her-name knew what was going through Esther's head, she would not be asking her opinion on what she thought about anything. At the moment, she could not recall the name of the futuristic device with the illuminated screen that the woman uses like a torch to light against the darkness inside the gym. So making decisions on the direction of their near future is foolish.

"Whatever will be will be," Esther replies with a shrug.

What's-her-name smiles instead of giving Esther a frown. Ether takes that as successfully pulling off her con. She doesn't need anyone knowing she is losing her marbles. If this is some sort of crisis situation, they would leave behind an addled old woman in a heartbeat to save themselves. The only thing more terrifying than being amongst people and gadgets that are all so confusing is being alone. Sometimes, Esther just stands in one place for long minutes when no one else is around because she cannot remember what she ought to do next and she needs interaction with someone to trigger her next task. If they leave her alone, she might stand in one place until she starves.

"My mother used to sing me a song when I was little," What's-her-name says. "Doris Day. '*Que sera, sera. Whatever will be, will be. The future's not ours to see. Que sera, sera.*' Somehow, she was able to make tomorrow seem beautiful."

They are both silent for a moment. Neither of the women seems to think today that there is anything beautiful about tomorrow.

"I'll make sure you're safe, Esther. Don't you worry."

She puts her dark hands over Esther's white, wringing fingers and steadies them. Her brown eyes meet Esther's. Esther has trouble meeting anyone's gaze lately, afraid they will see the truth of the scrambled workings behind her eyes. But What's-her-name is able to command a connection for long seconds.

"I'm sorry. I don't remember your name, dear," Esther says.

What's-her-name smiles kindly. She looks scared, but fear has not diluted compassion. So many of the folks in the gym stand alone, hugging themselves and feeling sorry, checking their glowing devices every ten seconds like salvation is coming on an LED screen. But the fearless few make their way around the room, taking measure, checking in, making plans.

"It's Rhonda," What's-her-name replies.

"Rhonda," Esther tries, and it seems right, like she should have known. Then softly, embarrassed: "I might forget."

"Of course," Rhonda replies. She still has her dark hands over Esther's pale ones. Rhonda squeezes. "Just remember one thing: if the white comes, you run, girl. You find something fixed and firm in the distance, and you run toward it without looking back."

Esther nods. She has been running from the white ever since she got lost walking around her neighborhood and had to ask a teenage boy with more pimples than piercings which was the way back to Everwood Street. She knew about finding something fixed, holding on to that anchor. Her husband. Her memories of her mother and brothers. Clarice.

Then the roof rips off, and up and away is white and white and white.

Stampede. What's-her-name disappears under a wave of panicked people. Her hands separate from Esther as they are both shoved backward, the bigger woman in yoga pants and sweatshirt running faster than she seemed capable of. Esther is pushed, pulled, and somehow finds herself outside, feeling lucky to not be trampled. The wind whips, the cold is crisp, and the white is everywhere. Her thin skin turns instantly numb. The wind steals her breath, and she feels like she is suffocating. Everyone else has been swallowed by the blowing snow. Esther is alone.

How long before the cold causes frostbite? Minutes? Moments? Not long, Esther is sure. Shivering, breath ragged, the chill already numbing fingers and ears and nose, she knows no one is going to find her if she just stays standing in one spot. So she moves forward. The cold is so bad it hurts, like being cut by a blade, over and over and over. White, white, more white, and then she sees the light.

-13°

Zack stares up into the sky, wind cutting across his wide, pimply face, pellets of snow pinging against his skin, frost collecting on his fuzzy eyebrows, ice forming on the fringes of his eyes, lips, and crusting around his nostrils. His mother's voice whispers on the wind: "Quit your whining, Zakaria. You're the man of the house, so try acting like one." But they are the words of a ghost, as his mother is most likely dead.

What the fuck just happened?

He had followed Trevin and Alex through the white. He had planned on dying in the basement and wasn't dressed for a wintry walkabout, so he had wrapped himself up in a blanket from the resort room, the same bedding his mother would have washed had Armageddon not rearranged the requirements of Mrs. Alaoui's job.

Trevin and Alex asked Zack where to get a snowmobile or an arctic cat. The garage that once stood out back of the northeast wing was just gone, removed as if it had never even existed. Zack had passed it on the way out of the hole in the ground where the pipe exited the basement, the cast iron ripped away like someone had carefully disconnected the joint and hauled away everything that had just recently existed aboveground. He had to feel along the wall to stay grounded in all the white, but suddenly the wall just ended. No more garage. No more vehicles.

They needed to find another way down the mountain.

"Where else can we find something that can get through this snow?" Trevin had asked.

"The school," Zack had suggested.

Zack remembered one severe storm a couple of winters ago where Mr. Galvin, the part-time school custodian and full-time resort handy-man, had to rescue a bunch of teenagers who had gone up to Lovers' Bluff for a Saturday night tryst and got stuck up there during a bad blizzard. (Bad, but not as bad as this one. This was the worst.) Mr. Galvin had taken a vehicle with tracks like a tank and a cab shaped like a bullet up the slope and came back in time for the underage forni-cators to attend Mass on Sunday morning.

So the trio had made their way to the school. Zack had followed the chain link fence that connected one corner of the resort that was still standing to the north wall of the garage at Zukunft Falls High School. There was a fleet of winter vehicles inside: trucks with snow tires as big as Zack is round, a school bus with chains on its wheels, snowmobiles with enclosed cabs, and the bullet-tank that Zack remem-bered: a black contraption with Blizzcat written in red on the side. There were no keys in any of them.

"Inside," Zack had suggested. "I suppose they keep the keys in the office."

So they found themselves inside the school, where a few hundred other people had also found shelter. Suddenly, community trumped escape. Trevin insisted on looking for someone named David. Alex just sighed and followed. Zack wandered around the gymnasium look-ing for his mother.

It was a kaleidoscope congregation, people Zack knew who worked at the resort, tourists he had never seen before, folks from town, stu-dents from his school, even Mr. Galvin, who let them in from the hall-way connecting to the garage and seemed in charge of regulating entry into the gymnasium. Zack had asked everyone he recognized if they'd seen his mother.

"Maristar?" Zack whispered when he'd seen a girl he recognized, shoulders shuddering as she wept softly in a corner. She'd been sitting near the banners that announced school sports' records: track, basketball, football, volleyball. Signs that might as well have said to kids like Zack: "You'll never be good enough." Her elbows had been on her knees, head hung between crossed arms. Her blonde hair had been hanging in her face, but Zack had known it was Maristar because she still wore her letter jacket with her last name over the number 10. She was a perfect ten. And she was all alone.

Zack had plopped down beside Maristar. Always confident, always in charge, always bitchy, he had never seen her vulnerable. Here she was, as scared and lonely as Zack.

"I was so frightened by the dark when I was little," Zack had said, sitting so close their knees almost touched. "My mom always told me there was nothing to be afraid of. When you look close, there is nothing there. She told me to be brave. But it didn't help. I was still scared. And now, out there, it is lunchtime, the sun shining somewhere beyond all that blowing snow. I look outside, and there is nothing but white. The opposite of the black that terrified me as a kid. My mom was right all along. It isn't what hides in the blackness that I needed to worry about. It is what hides in the white."

"Can you just shut the fuck up, Gurp?" Maristar had snapped, looking up, tears wetting her face but doing it in such a beautiful way. "I am trying to vlog my last days on Earth, and you are ruining my flow."

"I—" Zack had stammered. "I'm sorry. I was just trying to—"

"Did you think we were going to be friends now that Armageddon arrived? This isn't a goddamn movie, Gurp. People like me don't all of a sudden get the feels for people like you. Even if you were the last fucking guy on the planet, I wouldn't let you get within a hundred feet of my—"

And then the roof had ripped off the top of the gymnasium as if the school was an Amazon package and someone was really excited to see what was inside. One wall had fallen away entirely, opening the insides to the blizzard.

Maristar was up and running before Zack could scream. She had disappeared into the white, sprinting. *Run, Maristar*, Zack thought. *Because we are all ugly and cold on the inside, but at least you are super hot on the outside.* Zack thought that everyone ought to try and preserve the pretty things of this world.

Then Trevin was there, grabbing a fistful of shirt and yanking Zack to his feet. "C'mon, kid! Stick close!" Alex was on his heels. Zack followed. As fast as he could. He tried to stay close.

Now Zack is in the white, white everywhere, and the fright he felt as a fat little boy so scared of the dark was nothing compared to the stark terror of facing whitewhitewhite. The wind howls, like a banshee warning of imminent death. The flakes are like little knives, slicing him up just like the blades of the razor cut his folds of flesh when he tries to scrape away the downy stubble from his neck. The cold is extreme, reaching into his chest and forming icicles in his aorta. He wants to stop and curl up in a ball and cry and cry and cry.

His mother keeps him going: "Quit your whining, Zakaria. You're the man of the house, so try acting like one."

His mother and Trevin: "Hustle, kid! Move it!"

What the fuck is happening?

Tears prickle his eyes and then turn to ice at the edges. Zack sees the shadows of some of the other refugees from the gym. They form and fade behind the white veil of snow, the shifting blizzard revealing and concealing with every gust of wind. Zack would rather not witness the plight of his fellow man. He only needs to see Trevin. Trevin is the only one paying attention to whether Zack lives or dies. These strangers in the white disappear without Zack ever knowing their names: an old man running as fast as he can and still slower than Zack, a woman carrying a baby, a kid not much younger than Zack dragging her right leg like it is lame, a fierce-looking black man carrying someone and still outpacing Zack by double. Then there are the people he knows: Mr. Galvin, who gave up on guarding doors once the ceiling was gone;

Serafin May, who runs the diner; Harry Chan, from the resort; Delvin Mook, who is homeschooled and perhaps more ridiculous than even the Gurp. As he sees these fleeing folks both familiar and foreign, half of them disappear into the distance, concealed by the veil of white. The other half disappear *upward. SKYWARD*. Something plucks them up off the ground like human-sized daisies cultivated by a gardener as gargantuan as God. Each one screams as they ascend, as if the rapture is actually some horrific fate perpetrated by colossal monsters and Heaven above is really a terrible hell. The white swallows their screams before whatever is up there in the sky ends it another way.

Up and up, one after another. And none come back down.

Zack runs. He runs into the white. More white. Then more white.

What the fuck is going to happen next?

-14°

Aspen Wang comes to and wishes she would just pass out all over again. She likes the black better than the white.

Her mother had always scolded her for blurting out the inappropriate whenever she got nervous. When Aspen was eight, her mother had taken her to a black tie affair where Dr. Xueman Wang was being presented with a medical award for some breakthrough accomplishment that had saved a billion lives and would revolutionize *blahblahblah*, and her mother had introduced Aspen to the Chairman of the Board at the hospital. Aspen had tittered when he shook her hand, and she told him, "Sorry, I get the burps from escargot." On her first make-out session, with Savin Rutherford, Aspen had told him that the Chapstick in his front pocket was making her uncomfortable, and he had said he didn't have any Chapstick, and then she had said, "Well, then you have a really small dick." When Polly Andrison had made fun of her for not having a dad while they were on their senior high ski trip, Aspen had told Polly that at least she hadn't gone eighteen years believing Mr. Andrison was her biological father when it was really Mr. Randall, their high school soccer coach. Aspen had heard the chaperones gossiping about it in the hot tub earlier in the day. But Polly had never known until the senior high ski trip.

So when Aspen comes around to wicked cold, unending white, and the world whirling around her, she wishes she was still unconscious in the blackness rather than wide awake in white. Aspen blurts out, "Once you go black, you don't go back."

"Pardon?" asks a baritone voice borne on the wind.

Aspen is being carried like a baby, cradled in arms that seemed to exert no more effort than if she was an actual infant. The man has a crazy beard of black bristle shot with gray in a combination of age and hoarfrost. His head is covered in a hat made of fur and fowl, covering hair like a wild tangle of bent black and white wire. His eyes are embers against the cold, a gaze like that of a beast in the wild, more protector than predator.

Like Simba, the lion.

What is happening? Where is Mom? The last thing Aspen remembers is the hotel coming apart all around her. Walls had fallen in. The roof hadn't really collapsed. It had *disappeared*. Ripped away as if by a tornado. Then the floor had given way right from under her, and her last thought had been that she would die before she had made her mother proud. Too late. Then the black had swallowed her from underneath.

But that hadn't been the end of it, had it? The darkness had peeled away as if she was the pit of a fruit and someone had pried away the outside, revealing the center. Aspen had lain so still, staring up as the resort eroded around her. Instead of wanton destruction, it was as if something had purposefully taken it apart. Had disassembled it like the hotel was made of interlocking blocks and someone had been told to put their toys away. Hadn't Aspen seen what it was? Had she not stared right at it as it took the world away, piece by piece? Without the deliberate effort to dismantle, she would have been buried under tons of rubble. It had saved her. It was impossible. It was white. And she cannot picture it. Her mind rebels at the memory.

"Sorry," Aspen whispers to the burly black man.

He leans in, closer than she has ever been to a boy without it ending with a kiss. The erratic hair around his mouth tickles her lips as he answers, "Hold tight." He does not seem to have taken offense at her rather racist outburst.

She holds tight.

He dodges left and right, and through the white, she sees a man who reminds her of Mr. Rivers, their mailman. He disappears *upward*, sucked away like a crumb fallen victim to a dustbuster. Aspen shoves down a scream. As the big man races across an alabaster oblivion, Aspen looks over his shoulder. She can't see any more than ten feet in any direction: front, back, left, right, up. Behind them, a larger woman in yoga pants and a sweatshirt advertising Patel's Pilates is plucked off the ground as if she weighs nothing instead of too much. Aspen and her rescuer run past an elderly couple trying to help each other navigate the white, each pointing in the opposite direction, neither pointing up, which is where they both end up an instant later. The man carrying Aspen does not run in a straight line, but rather he zigzags like he is running football drills. A kid somewhat younger than Aspen overtakes them and sprints past in a straight line. He turns, eyes meeting Aspen's, and his mouth forms the word "Help" before he is snatched off the ground. The sound is carried away by the wind and muffled by the snow. The boy is gone. The sky takes him away.

The man carrying Aspen stops zigzagging. There is a tall fellow, someone with the height and build of a professional basketball player, standing still in an expensive purple suit and fancy violet shoes that afforded no protection whatsoever against the white or anything in it. He looks ridiculous considering the circumstances. Shivering uncontrollably, hugging himself and rocking back and forth, he stares off in the opposite direction, lost. Aspen's rescuer runs toward him from behind, and Aspen is terrified for the tall man. He must be the next victim. Somehow, her rescuer knows who is next. Then, just as they arrive near the basketball baller, their approach unnoticed downwind and muffled by the snow, her rescuer stops, hunches, tucking Aspen into a ball.

Aspen, one eye peeking out from the man's large, enveloping arms, sees the basketball baller through the furry edges of the bearskin parka she is wrapped in. Something yanks the tall baller up and away. Her rescuer did not warn the victim. He used the baller as bait.

Without wasting a moment, the grizzled man launches them forward, twenty paces before a shape suddenly looms out of the white. It is a diner featuring a black and orange sign that says "Open" hanging on the glass front door, although when the burly man hits it, it gives him momentary pause before the lock snaps and they are inside. They tumble to the tile floor as her rescuer loses balance from the unexpected and temporary resistance of the dead-bolted door.

Aspen is dizzy and weak. Three of her fingers are still numb, and as she gets her first lungful of warm air, she starts on a coughing fit that lasts for at least a minute. She sees the man who saved her stand up and look across the room at two dozen folks crouched behind the lunch counter, peering from behind like soldiers in battle peeking over the lip of a trench. Over the bark of her hacking, Aspen hears one of the men hiding in the diner tell her rescuer to "shut your bitch up." Through tears from her wracking coughs, she sees the blurry, burly man draped in dead animals step between Aspen and the man who spoke.

Her coughs finally subside enough to hear the back and forth.

"All this noise is going to draw that...thing to where we are hiding."

"Hiding? It knows where we are, you idiot."

"You broke the door, Mountain Man," a woman accuses. She wears a waitress uniform with an "Annette" name tag. "Oh yeah, I know who you are. You live up in the cabin on the bluff. Roman somethin' or other. The kids call you the Mountain Man."

"What are you trying to keep out?" Roman asks, ignoring the waitress. "That lock couldn't even stop me, so what do you think it will do for something so big? It can demolish buildings as easily as a wrecking ball. When that thing in the white wants us, it will get us."

"We need to run," someone else says, an overweight teen flanked by two young men dressed in expensive and flashy ski attire.

"We need to stay," Roman disagrees. "It's feeding now. Plucking the easy prey. It only wrecks the buildings when it needs materials."

"You know what it is?" Annette interrogates Roman like she thinks this is somehow his fault.

"It doesn't matter what it is," Roman says dismissively. "It just matters what it wants."

"You know how this thing thinks, Mountain Man?" asks another fellow, dressed in a suit with the airs of a politician.

"It thinks like any other predator," Roman replies, his voice a constant monotone grumble. "Food, food, food."

"What does it need the materials for then?" asks Annette. "Building a cabin of its own?"

"Building a trap. For food," Roman answers. "For us."

And Aspen starts off on another coughing fit. She can hardly breathe. Her lungs burn. She prays for mercy, that she might pass out again. She longs for the black to return.

-15°

The school is razed, just like the hotel. If Xueman Wang recollects correctly from their drive into town, these two buildings would account for the two largest structures in the resort area. If some massive, mindless beast is destroying Zukunft Falls in a tantrum à la Godzilla attacking Tokyo, then the pattern ought to be random or instinctual. This suggests logic.

Already cold, Xueman becomes colder.

What the hell is that thing out there in the white?

They witnessed the very end of the educational institution's Armageddon. Xueman and David had thrown themselves backward, into a frosty bank that bordered the playground on the east side like they were making snow angels, so they'd had front-row seats to the devastation. Something concealed by the blizzard had plucked away entire sections of the school, shadowed shapes moving like staticky images on a television that wasn't tuned. Walls had been erased in the white like images on a shaken Etch-A-Sketch. Then the desks, equipment, debris, and detritus had disappeared, scooped up by something unseen. Carried up and gone, as if by an albino digger camouflaged by a snowstorm.

"What did you see?" David asks as they stand on a floor that used to be a basketball court, the free-throw line under Xueman's feet.

"Nothing," she answers.

She is not sure if that made her frustrated or relieved.

David is looking at footprints quickly being erased by snow and wind, like the surf wiping away with every wave that breaks onshore any evidence of a beach expedition.

"There were a lot of people in here," David assesses. "They scattered in every direction."

Xueman scans the smattering of footprints as though she might recognize Aspen's amongst them before they all disappear. She is sure her daughter is still alive. She just doesn't know where to look for her.

She stares into the wind, face freezing. It is colder than she has ever experienced. But it gets a lot colder in many places on the globe, and people survive. People always survive. Her daughter is out there in the white, and Xueman will lean into the wind and cold and she will find her. She pulls up the collar on the ski mask she took from the equipment shed, claps her thick mittens together, and stomps her boots to keep the blood flowing in her feet.

Somewhere in the distance, thunder sounds, that unnatural crack that portends something other than lightning. It may be close, but she thinks it is far. She is a doctor. She uses reason and knowledge to make a diagnosis. The thing in the white is taking apart the largest places first. It must be using the raw material from the buildings for something else. Something that is not right here. For the moment, Xueman deduces she and David are safe.

But just for this moment.

The thunder claps again.

"God sounds the baritone dirge that signals the doom of the world," David says.

"Something your grandmother used to tell you during a storm?" Xueman guesses.

"Nope. Just made it up, Doc," David replies, looking off into the direction of the signal of doom.

Xueman nods. She lives by logic, and David by poetry. They would both die the same if the thing in the white returns.

"How well do you know this town?" she asks David.

David wears a fancy ski jacket and snow pants with bright blue boots, flashy but functional. The temperature is deadly, and they have just enough defense to survive the cold for a while. He has one arm duct-taped to his torso, and the other has an ice pick attached to it. Trussed and weaponized, he looks like some kind of cyborg soldier made for arctic battle. He has a wisp of a mustache and a little more hair on his chin, both catching frost and making him look a little like a Hispanic Colonel Sanders. Like a mother straightening her son's collar, Xueman reaches over and pulls up his mask until just his eyes peer through, slits against the wind.

"We went bar hopping, which amounted to hopping from the first bar to the only other bar in this little town," David says in a voice muffled by material and snow.

"Did you notice any other large buildings? Besides the resort and the school?"

"It was my bachelor party, so I wasn't really paying attention. After the first bar, I could barely see my hand in front of my face let alone any other businesses on the block. And it was because of booze, not a blizzard." David squints against the white, as if he is trying to see the smattering of homes and businesses around them. They might as well have been in the middle of Antarctica. "I saw a church. I told Trevin, my fiancé, 'That'd be a great place to be married.' It was mostly a joke. He looked terrified." David pauses. Xueman wonders, *Just remembering his missing fiancé, or just realizing something about that moment?* "It was a big church. Between the two bars."

"We need to warn whoever is in that church," Xueman says. "Aspen might be taking shelter there. Or Trevin. We need to tell them that the church is the next target."

"Are you sure?"

"Sure enough. Can you find it?"

David is still staring into the white. If he is afraid of something grabbing him from the veil of snow, he is not showing it. He nods. "Yeah." He doesn't sound too sure.

They move forward. Things glide by them in the white, like victims wandering around the smoky destruction of a battlefield, in shock, lost even though many of them must call Zukunft Falls home. Xueman is startled every time a body passes her in the blizzard. Sometimes they are close enough to reach out and grab her before she even sees them. Other times, they are just shadows out of sight, like silhouettes passing behind a white sheet flapping in the breeze. She thinks each one might be Aspen for a moment, but she is always disappointed. She thinks everyone might be the monster out there in the white coming to pluck her away, but she is always wrong. So far.

David puts his face near her ear and shouts over an extended gust of wind. "Do you hear that?"

Xueman pauses. She is bundled with everything she has been able to cobble together since something disassembled the hotel. Earmuffs she found discarded in the snow and her cinched hood dull every sound except for the constant wailing wind and the occasional clap of mysterious thunder. She tilts her head against the worst of the wind and listens. The storm seems to be saying something if you listen closely to the changes and characteristics of the gusts. Terrible things. Like the Devil himself warning of impending doom. Like an imp that brags about taking your daughter, never to be seen again. Then something, beyond the edge of nature.

A growl. Like a cougar or a bear. Maybe some predator from the mountains came to town to join the party. Cornered and confounded by the inexplicable, perhaps Xueman's untimely end would come at the claws of a completely tangible and territorial mountain lion. The sound seems to swell and soften, comes nearer, then fades away. The weather plays tricks on directions and distance.

"Move," David hollers.

He shoves Xueman backward, hard. She flies off her feet, the skinny young man possessing impressive strength for someone half-lame and trussed like a Thanksgiving turkey. She sees lights come out of the white, bearing down on David. Xueman has time to recognize a large pickup jacked up almost high enough for David to duck under. It swerves at the last second, missing her only companion in this chaos by mere millimeters. Then it disappears into the blizzard, two red tail-lights slowly swallowed by the white until they are gone.

"They're going to run right into something or somebody," Xueman says as David helps her to her feet.

"Desperation," David answers over the wail of wind.

She takes his one good hand, her swollen woolen mitten in his nylon and neoprene glove, and squeezes. "Gumption," she repeats; it has become their own personal rally cry. "Let's get to that church."

David nods. "Maybe God has some answers about all of this."

-16°

Evergreen.

The jade boughs break up the white and block the wind, giving Rhonda brief respite from the world on the other side of the trees. It is a little park in the center of town. She remembers passing it on the way to the resort. That seems like eons ago. She had been so eager to meet Howard. She had been so afraid of fifty. Now, Howard is like something that happened in the Stone Age, and fifty now appears iffy rather than inevitable. So terrified of growing old, Rhonda did not consider the alternative: never growing any older.

The heart of this copse of pine is preternaturally quiet, a respite from incomprehensible chaos. Instead of white bullets all around in a maelstrom, fluffy flakes float down like on a picturesque Christmas morning. It would have been idyllic if not for the interruption in the distance of the thunderous boom that signaled something unearthly existed at the edges of her reality.

The cold. Rhonda has never been so cold. Her breath puffs out in white and just hangs there, a bright cloud growing thicker and wider with each exhalation. The wind had stolen it away until she found this perfect shelter. Now her exhaust remains as proof of life, that she is still a breathing, living being. Each frozen cloud also exists as a warning that this world wants to turn everything to ice.

Rhonda had fled hastily from the gymnasium. Inside the gym, it had been cold enough to keep on her coat and hat, but she had removed her gloves as she made the rounds looking for Esther's companion. Now, her hands are plunged deep into her pockets and still the cold creeps through, like water slowly soaking into a roll of tissue: deeper and deeper and deeper until it is penetrated to the very core.

She still has her scarf from Howard. Rhonda pulls it up over her nose, half numb, with fingers she can't feel anymore. The thought of frostbite frightens her. She pulls her arms into her coat and shoves her hands into her armpits, praying to a God she has mostly ignored all her life to spare her the fate of amputation.

Rhonda had lost Esther; that would have made her cry if not for fear of icicles forming from her eye sockets. She had just told the addled old woman, "I'll make sure you're safe." Then discord. Stampede. Survival. Now peace. And cold.

She cannot stay here, but to leave the shelter of the trees means wind and white and whatever is out there in the snow. In every direction now, there is green frosted in white, gentle lines and comforting color, like a pastoral painting hanging in a bank lobby. This isn't real. This is not life. Life is the unknown, the unpleasant, cold and white and windy.

Rhonda peers out between boughs, staring into oblivion. The white has erased everything. She does not know how far the borders of the park extend. Even if she did, the homes beyond might be as gone as the resort and the school. Something had razed those buildings as if it had been harvesting raw materials to reconstitute into some superstructure. What if the thing in the white decides it needed fresh timber? Rhonda looks up and around at the green. Suddenly, she thinks the copse may act as a green traffic light signaling something to go ahead, a glowing patch of color in the white like a beacon to colossal beasts.

Something might be staring back from the white right now. The world is unfixed, like Rhonda exists inside a cosmic Etch-A-Sketch and God is shaking, shaking, shaking. Perhaps this is His twenty-first-century version of the Flood, erasing the world and starting anew. Would He bother with an ark this time around? Would He give a third chance to humanity or just give up? Certainly, a fifty-year-old woman past the point of reproduction probably wouldn't make the cut.

Rhonda had never been one to wait for divine intervention. When the wrinkles had started to wreck her face, she'd taken action. When her tits had started to sag, she'd made things right. When the gray had invaded like a disease, she'd fought back. As fifty approached, she had embraced denial and wallowed in mistruth. No one was going to save her tragically sagging backside for her, so she had to save her own ass.

Things move in the Etch-A-Sketch world, forming then unforming, shadows passing like ships in a fog. "Hello?" she calls, but no one stops. Perhaps the wind carries her words away; probably everyone is running for their life and damn stopping for conversation. Or maybe the smaller things in the white are no more human than the massive monster dismantling the town building by building is.

Like creatures of the forest both big and small, perhaps these invaders have things the relative size of bears (represented on the mountain in Mothra-sized dimensions) and things the proportional size of chipmunks (which might make them the same size as people, matching the shadows passing just outside the edge of definition). Rhonda stops calling out to the shadowy shapes. She does not know what is all out there in the white.

At the perimeter of the small copse, she stands, petrified. Frozen. If she waits much longer, she will be ice, indeed. The temperature continues to drop.

When Rhonda finds herself hesitating for too long, she just jumps. She had been reluctant to start online dating, so she had just sat down one day and entered her info, pressed send. She'd had second thoughts about this trip to Montana, so she had just booked the flight and the room and hadn't looked back. Howard had ended up being a bust, but instead of retreat, she had stayed at the resort. Now, Rhonda pushes her arms back into her sleeves, hands into pockets, and steps out into the white, leaving behind the safety of the trees, looking for civilization rather than the comfort of solitary shelter.

Direction is deceiving. It is alike everywhere she turns. She forges forward. Hands that had blessedly warmed up again start to slowly lose feeling. Rhonda flinches from moving shadows, imagining human-sized chipmunks with razor teeth moving past her. Frosted vampires. Undead predators. Maybe the monolithic monsters instead are mythic frost giants from some Scandinavian lore and the scurrying shadows in the white are their minions, scampering about for carrion like little carnivorous birds pecking the bones of a lion's kill

She wonders if the soughing air is wind or breath.

Is the wailing sound the blizzard or someone screaming?

Is the white just snow and sleet or something sinister, ready to reach out and end her?

Rhonda pushes on, forward, through. A shadow looms before her, something larger than the other silhouettes passing in the white, towering up so high it disappears into the white and wide enough to disappear to her left and right. The shadow sways back and forth like it moves to some earthly beat akin to the pull of the tides. Then the shadows gain color. Green. Rhonda has found another copse of pines.

She pushes into the calm center made by the thick, heavy boughs, looking for someone who has taken shelter in the woods just as she had. Inside, she finds footprints leading in and leading out. The same prints she makes as she enters. It is the same set of trees. Rhonda has managed to walk in a circle.

The world works against her.

She exits the same way as she entered, her prints disappearing off to her right, erased by snow and wind. This time, she forges to her left, trying to adjust course so she does not make another circle counterclockwise.

The shadows come and go. None stop. Neither Rhonda nor anyone she crosses. She is looking for civilization, not other solitary strangers. Or otherworldly creatures. She worries that alien beings have inhabited her world, but as she stumbles forward in a world of white, nothing definite and direction undetermined. She wonders if maybe this isn't her world anymore. White, everywhere. People, nowhere? Maybe Rhonda is the one who is trespassing, and now this is *their* world.

-17°

Lost.

The white turns them around. Doc is a tourist and David doesn't know this town any better than she does. They are looking for the church, but God is as lost in the white as the rest of them. David once believed that the Almighty would light the way through the darkest of times, but darkness was never really the test. White is the test. And even God fails to fill in the blank.

"This isn't the right way," Doc says as they pass the post office for the third time, half her words whipped away in a wail of wind.

"C-c-cold," David manages. Then Doc's masked face is looking up at him, her dark eyes peering through the narrow slit in the material protecting her skin.

"We need a break from the blizzard," Doc says, a mix of medicine and meteorology.

David points with his ice pick, like a long metal finger picking a place to port, to the pub next to the post office. "There." A neon light in the window advertises spirits, a respite for souls in the storm. David recognizes the place. It is the bar where he had celebrated with Trev. The whole wedding party had been drinking last night. It seems a lifetime ago. David recalls the way Alex had been looking at Trev, the way he always looked at Trevin, and David becomes even colder.

Inside, the bar is dimmer than David remembers. Darker. Candles flicker in wax poured into several shot glasses lined up along the bar top. The flames serve as the sole source of illumination. The jukebox that had previously played a steady stream of Streisand last night is now quiet, the shadows dancing along the wall moving to some silent sound. There had not been an open seat some twelve hours ago, but now just one stool is occupied. The endless flow of liquor when David and his friends had been here has become a single finger of warm whiskey poured by a solitary alcoholic.

The drunkard saddled up to the bar is an old man in a deputy's uniform. His badge catches in the flickering candlelight as he puts his empty shot glass in a row already numbering more than a dozen. David is still shivering, and the whiskey looks shimmering, the color of warmth. Without asking, Doc strolls across to where the solitary patron hunches over his booze and takes the bottle. She pours six ounces in an empty stein and hands it to David.

"Just what the doctor ordered?"

"It'll warm you up," Doc says.

David drinks the elixir, and it is better than any damn medicine. The warmth flows down his throat and spreads to his whole body in an instant. He can't imagine anything in any hospital that could have been more effective.

"And what's your story?" Doc asks the deputy, who looks like he hasn't even registered the new arrivals. "I see a badge. Shouldn't you be out there serving and protecting?"

The old man turns and looks at David and Doc, finally realizing he is no longer alone. His eyes are glazed over by layers and layers of inebriation. This guy must have been drinking since the resort was attacked.

"The shituation out there ish shome kinda Hollywood shhhit," the deputy slurs. "Do I look like Duane the fuck Johnshon?"

"Does that work for doctors, too?" Doc challenges. "Can I just sit out the apocalypse because I don't have any balls?"

Anger clears up his speech. His gaze comes out of the haze a little. "Listen, lady, I fought in the goddamn war. I served my country. Thirty years. I got out, and I just wanted a simple job working security up in the mountains. At a fancy resort. I didn't sign up for fuckin' monsters."

"People are dying out there."

"People are going to die whether I am out there or in here," the deputy says. "And it is cold out there."

"You could give it a damn try," Doc sneers.

The old man holds up another shot glass, staring at the way the candlelight flickers in the amber sauce. He is shaking. He downs it before he spills a drop.

"So who is it?" the deputy asks.

"What are you talking about?"

"You have someone you love out there," he says. He looks from Doc to David. "Both of you."

Doc looks away. David nods. "My fiancé. Her daughter."

"Well, I got nobody I love out there. They're down in SoCal, in the sun, nice and warm. I pray to God that the white never gets there."

"A blizzard in Southern California? Just what the hell are you talking about, mister?"

"It's moving south," the old man informs. He points at a cell phone set at the end of the row of empty shot glasses. "You see, I did my job for a minute. When the resort was demolished, I called into the sheriff's office down the mountain. He already turned it over to the military. The sheriff told me straight up, 'No one's coming for you, Deacon.' He was instructed to stand down by the United States Army. So I still have some buddies in the service. I called an old friend we called Junkyard. Junkyard's answer was that everything is FUBAR."

"If the military is involved, there must be a rescue mission coming," Doc says.

Deacon the deputy shrugs. "Junkyard said radar is ineffective in this white. Visibility is zero. Infrared, ultraviolet, x-ray: none of it is working in this particular snowstorm. They can't fly a plane in it. They can't send troops in to fight what they can't see. They can't shoot a missile at the fuckin' monster if they can't aim."

"What about tanks? Troops with some conventional guns? Rescue operation? Evacuation support?"

"They set up a perimeter down the slope at the edge of the white," Deacon says. "But coming up the mountain would be suicide. They sent one squad, heavily armed, and they were erased like a bad drawing."

"They can't leave us here to die," Doc argues.

Deacon sighs, shaking his head like she was a toddler trying to understand complex politics. "Collateral losses."

"Do they know what it is?" David asks.

Deacon looks at him, and David wishes he had never asked. The look in the old man's eyes is worse than fear. Worse than confusion. It is knowing something that you cannot understand. It is staring into the face of an unavoidable end.

"Junkyard told me what he knows. There were a bunch of scientists in the mountains working on a way to prove that global warming is a hoax. They tried a method they thought was pretty damn clever: they tried to use wormholes or tachyons or some science-y shit to take samples of the atmosphere from the future. Crazy bastards. They ripped open a tear into tomorrow. Junkyard said something came through. A fucking beast a hundred feet tall. Defies biology. Rewrites the playbook on physics. It came through with the storm. Snow and cold like nothing we know." Deacon blinks in a slow and bleary gesture. "I guess those fuckin' eggheads were right. Global warming is a joke. Ha. Ha."

"That sounds like bullshit," Doc says. "The military is probably just covering over something they screwed up."

"Maybe," Deacon discounts with a shrug. "Maybe they know just what it is. Maybe they are doing secret experiments now that will make terrible things tomorrow. Maybe it is all just a lie and it is really an alien invasion. Or a prehistoric beast from the dinosaur age. That thing is going to kill us all, no matter where or when it came from."

"Whatever it is, and wherever it came from, it isn't going to get my daughter," Doc says. "So you can sit and soak and die, or you can try to survive."

"Indeed," Deacon agrees, pouring another shot and lifting it in salute. "But it is warm and toasty in here. And it is too goddamn cold out there."

So Deacon stays. And David and Doc return to the bitter cold.

-18°

Roman faces antagonistic faces.

There was a reason he had left civilization. It was becoming too uncivilized.

Things have not rebounded in his twenty years of exile. The looks he is getting reflect the general dissolution of culture that he had observed accelerating in the years prior to his exodus. Everyone looks at small, handheld television screens every five seconds like the devices could somehow save them from Armageddon. No one talks *to* one another but rather *at* each other, as if social mores have devolved to the point that everyone speaks a different language and the contraptions in their hands are the only things that can translate. But the machines aren't going to save them. Salvation is not made of wire and glass.

He would rather deal with the monster in the white. Roman can at least understand the hunt, the dance between predator and prey.

"It is some ancient colossus that was unearthed by an avalanche," suggests some pencil-pushing geek that looks like he might cry at the next sound of the baritone boom.

"Stay off the blogs, dude. Lies and lies. My cousin upstate is posting that no one knows shit."

"It is science," says a grumpy old bastard. "Science gone mad."

"This is God's work," whispers a wide woman. "The reaping is upon us."

"The news is reporting that the creature emerged from a tear in space and time," informs a teenage girl that does not even look up from her glowing phone. "They say it is some sort of arctic dinosaur."

Roman has been stuck in this diner with these idiots for a half an hour, and he is already willing to take his chances with whatever is out in the white rather than suffer one more endless utterance of these absolute imbeciles. Everyone has become an expert on everything while Roman has been away these last twenty years, as if the empty electronics they clutch in their fists have told them they are all geniuses but taught them nothing. If not for Aspen, he might have left these refugees to fend for themselves. But between coughing fits, the young woman told Roman that she is a tourist from Portland, Oregon. This was to be the last mother–daughter trip before Aspen graduates in the Spring and moves to Massachusetts. Aspen will not leave without her mother, and Roman will not leave without Aspen.

"It is not something old," Roman says. "We are not dealing with frostosaurs or resurrected mammoths."

"How the hell do you know?" asks the son of a bitch who looks like a politician.

"Because I know the things that hunt. I can tell you every animal out there in the wild. Evolution has made them smarter, faster, better than anything before. But even the best hunters, from falcons to cats to wild dogs, are not like that thing in the white. It is planning. It is building. It is laying a trap. That is not something so stupid as to have once gone extinct. It is something new."

"Maybe a mutation," suggests a fat kid with acne so bad Roman isn't sure of the natural color of his skin.

"Like the lizard that became Godzilla," agrees an effeminate fellow standing next to the boy.

"Did you see a nuke go off somewhere in the Rockies?" Aspen snaps, withering sarcasm that makes the fat kid blush like only a pretty young woman could.

Roman cannot explain it. This thing is smart. Smarter than anything he has ever seen hunt these wilds. Maybe alien. Or science has created some cloning calamity. He thinks again about *Jurassic Park*, where resurrecting prehistoric predators went horrifically wrong. This thing is more clever than velociraptors and more dangerous than a tyrannosaurus rex. This thing is setting a trap, like Roman hunting bears or beavers. Roman recalls the twenty-foot wall of debris he saw at the edge of where the resort had once stood. It is reusing demolished materials to build the wall. First, the resort. Then the school.

"What is the next largest building in town?" Roman asks.

"The Church of Ascension is the only other building bigger than City Hall," the posturing politician says.

"How much bigger?"

Like Roman is asking the size of his penis, the fellow seems almost offended by the question. "Twice. At least."

"You're the mayor?" Roman surmised.

"For the last thirty years. I am Saul Brick," Mayor Brick says. "You've lived a mile up the mountain for the last two decades and you don't know who I am?"

"I don't care," Roman replies. "The church is the next target."

"Reverend Elizabeth will have her congregation gathered there," says a waitress with a name tag that reads "Annette." "The devout will believe they are safe in the house of the Lord."

"Maybe they *are* safe there," suggests an old man who might have been to church a time or two in his day.

"You think God gives a fuck, old timer?" Roman says.

Monsters are ripping the town to shreds. People are like popcorn, gobbled up randomly. This weather is an unnatural, unending blizzard that mutes all distance. If God has any part of this, it is in ending the world in water once again. Just this time, He is going with frozen precipitation instead of rain.

"Someone needs to warn them," the fat kid suggests, concerned. Maybe he knows someone who might be hiding out at the church.

"We need to get the hell out of here," Mayor Brick overrides. "We can use the attack on the church as a distraction, and make our way out of town. If we stick together as a whole, then everyone in this diner can get out alive."

"Mayor *Prick*," Aspen attacks, "my mother is still out there. And other people's loved ones. You want us all to turn tail and leave them behind?"

"The mayor is right," comes the strutting asshole who wanted Roman to throw Aspen out into the white when she couldn't quit coughing. "We stay any longer looking for loved ones, and we all end up dead. Everyone else might already be out of town, safe and sound."

"Save our own ass and screw everyone else, huh?" Aspen says.

"My wife is out there, too, you little bitch," the bruiser snaps, hands clenching into fists. "But what good am I to her dead, toe jam to some fucking King Kong."

"You're just afraid she ran off without bothering to look for you," Roman says. "And she probably did. Now sit down and shut up. And if you call this young lady a bitch again, I will personally shove your ass out there into the white and you can deal with the thing out there all alone."

The bruiser snorts like a bull pissed and properly prodded, resigned to imminent castration, steered to proper behavior.

"You have a better idea, Mountain Man?" asks Annette.

"We send an envoy to the church. Warn them. Just a small group. If they get themselves into trouble, we don't want to lose everyone," Roman explains. "But a big enough squad in case the group gets attacked on the way, so there might be enough to get one or two through to warn the ones in the church."

"And the rest of us just wait here like sitting ducks?" Mayor Brick snorts.

"Some," Roman says. "It's safe here. For now. The church is next, then City Hall. This diner is small enough to offer safe shelter for the foreseeable future."

"The future is certainly not foreseeable," quips the pink-haired guy standing between the fat kid and a pouty Mexican fellow. Had Roman ever seen a man with pink hair? Maybe Boy George? When he exiled himself, the most outrageous thing around had been Madonna. Now, she was probably someone's grandmother.

"You say *some* of us should wait here," Mayor Brick says. "What about the rest?"

"I want to take a team to do a recon around the perimeter surrounding the town," Roman proposes. "The thing in the white is building a wall at least twenty feet high, and I think it might already extend most of the way around Zukunft Falls. I want to see if there is a way through the wall. Maybe it's incomplete, or perhaps there's a weak point. Before we just run for it, we need to survey an escape route. If we try to go up and over a twenty-foot-high wall, that thing will pick us off like plums from a full fruit tree."

Aspen steps up. "I'll go to the church."

The fat kid comes over and stands by Aspen, twice as wide but the same height. "Me, too."

The two homosexuals join the kid. "We need to find someone. He might be there."

A half dozen more locals join them.

The Mayor and the bruiser are amongst those standing with Roman.

Then a black woman bursts in the diner door, the bell above her head announcing her arrival. She looks as cold as ice itself. Ungloved hands emerge from her pockets, almost white despite being African American and shaking like an octogenarian in the throes of palsy. Her eyes sweep the room, skittering right over Roman and the rest. Not finding what she is looking for, she meets the Mountain Man's eyes. She just knows who is in charge.

"Going somewhere?" she asks, assessing the two groups heading toward the door.

"There are survivors at the church that need to be warned," Aspen says.

The black woman looks at the rest of the crowd cowering at the back half of the diner, huffing and puffing as if she had already run a

96

marathon and someone has asked her to join them on a decathlon. "Then someone give me some damn gloves," she swears. "I'm comin' with."

-19°

Esther sits in the front row of the church, listening to bullshit.

She looks left and right. No one else seems to see it. Now granted, her mind is as scrambled as Sunday morning eggs, but she knows a load of excreta when it slops on her shoes. Her problem is that no one in this conned congregation is going to leave with her to escape into the white, and if she goes back outside into the blizzard alone, she will likely lose her way and die from hypothermia.

Besides, these kindly Christian souls would never let a confused old woman leave of her own accord. She is their prisoner. For her own good. Even if it means her eventual death. At least they professed to prepare her everlasting soul for the great beyond.

A pastor preaches from the pulpit: "Into Your hands, we deliver ourselves, O Lord. Keep us safe in Your bosom and protect us from these minions of Satan razing our homes. Shield us from this evil wrath so that we may spread the deeds of Your love and mercy to our brothers and sisters across the world."

Candles light the interior, but it is the exterior that concerns Esther. Usually, she forgets things that are recent developments, but this thing is nearly unforgettable. A generator out back runs the heat, keeping the dropping temperatures at bay for the time being. The only other thing drawing electricity is the neon cross outside, atop the apex of the church roof like the lamp on a lighthouse, a bright beacon that lit Esther's way to shelter. It pierced the white veil more than any other thing still shining in this whole town. But if Esther could see it from half a block away, then so could the thing out there in the white.

"God will protect us from harm," the pastor promised when Esther warned that the glowing cross might attract the wrong kind of attention.

And everyone believes everything that this pastor utters.

So, adopted by a cult, protected against her will, Esther sits front and center, waiting with the congregation for an end to this situation. The rest of them believe that God will protect them through the crisis. Esther is sure that any minute the roof will rip away like a lid pulled off a can of almonds, all sorts of nuts inside just ready for the snacking.

The lengthy sermon is interrupted not by the dreadful thunder boom that sounds regularly somewhere out in the white, but rather an insistent banging on the front door, like a neighbor who has just caught your son shtupping his daughter. The pastor herself glides down the center aisle. Her hair is wound into a tight bun, her entire face a grimace, as if pulling the hair back yanked her expression taut. Esther appreciates her black robes, crisp and unfaded, counterpoint to the endless snow. The congregation, some seventy or eighty locals, watch her in awe as she moves serenely to answer the incessant knocking.

The pastor opens the door, the wind making the candles throughout the church flutter and dance. She converses with the newcomers but does not automatically allow them entry into God's house. If she is His bouncer, she is discerning about His guests. Esther gets up and wanders nearer the front door as the pastor's conversation escalates into a passionate exchange of words. Esther peers over the pastor's shoulder, into the blizzard. Two figures stand outside, nearly invisible in the unwavering snowstorm.

"God's house is no place for the Serpent's lies," the pastor suddenly shouts.

The Pastor is backing up from a snow-plastered intruder with an icepick duct taped to one wrist and his other arm incapacitated. He threatens her with the pointed end of his appendage. Several men in the congregation stand, the scrawny newcomer outnumbered ten to one.

Five to one. A petite figure follows the kid inside. She is carrying a chainsaw. Esther gets confused a lot nowadays, misremembering right from wrong or now from then, but she knows in any world of right and wrong, a woman in a church with a chainsaw is like a lunatic's guess in a round of a crazy game of Clue!

The woman is no more than five foot tall. She holds up a hand to warn off the men who started standing up to defend the pastor. She pulls back her hood and scans the congregation as if she is looking for someone in particular. Esther wonders as she often does, *Am I supposed to know her? Is she looking for me?* But the woman's gaze skips over Esther and moves on.

She gets to the end of the line of pews and looks disappointed. She shakes her head as if that could erase whatever she was hoping to find. The woman steps forward, her companion with the ice pick at her side. Standing at the end of the aisle, she addresses the congregation.

"My name is Xueman Wang. I am a doctor. My friend David and I think you are all in danger."

"God will provide," the pastor counters.

"The Lord helps those who help themselves," Dr. What's-her-name says back.

"The Prince of Lies turns turgid truth," the pastor declares.

"Just hear us out, lady," Dr. What's-her-name's companion pleads.

"Why do you think we are in danger?" Esther inquires. She is being held basically against her will. She doesn't belong here. She doesn't know anyone in this church, does she?

"Whatever the hell that thing is out there is taking buildings apart," the doctor explains. "It started with the resort. Then the school."

"The school?" cries a woman even older than Esther, as if she might have a loved one there.

The doctor looks at the worried old woman like she is delivering dire news to the family of a terminal patient.

"What sort of logic makes the leap that the devil destroying this town will move from tawdry resort to place of learning to the House of God?" the pastor asks.

"Opulence," the small woman dripping water in the vestibule says, looking around the ornate interior of the church. It is bigger than it needs to be, arch ceilings rising high to accommodate large and ridiculously rendered decor. In a small resort town, seating for four hundred is excessive. "After the hotel and the school, is this the next largest structure in town?"

The pastor does not answer.

Wasn't I at the school, Esther wonders? Tries to remember. There was something. Something in the white. The roof. The roof coming off. The cold. Alone. Wandering in the blizzard. She remembers seeing the cross.

The old woman worried about whoever had been at the school answers, "It is."

"We need to get out of here," Dr. What's-her-name says.

Esther tries to remember why, but it is already slipping away. She can't remember. But she knows she does not want to stay here anymore.

"Take me with you," Esther asks.

"Me, too," chimes the even older woman with someone special at the school.

"No," the pastor commands. The larger men of the congregation come forward as if she has asked them to usher. "No one is leaving. We have to believe firmly in the protection of God. If the devil senses weakness in the church, it might embolden an attack. We have to fortify our steadfastness."

"We have a fucking chainsaw, woman," the lad with the icepick argues. "We can cut a hole through the wall if you don't want to let us through the door."

"Too late," Esther declares. Even as her mind goes, her hearing inexplicably has sharpened. Old age almost always means the deterioration of all the senses, but maybe God decided to bestow some compensation to balance the loss of her memories. Or perhaps it is the devil, sensing weakness, emboldened, because preternatural hearing is maybe not a blessing. She hears the muffled thump of something heavy butting against the deep, thick fluff of snow right outside the stained glass windows. "It's here."

-20°

Alex Dove follows Trevin's footprints, putting his smaller soles in the imprint of Trevin's larger feet. He will follow Trev anywhere. Brave and bold, Trevin is going to find a way to keep them alive and get them out of this nightmare. If they find David, Trev can dump that bitch as soon as they escape this insane blizzard and whatever the fuck is stalking them in the white. Then Alex can have Trev all to himself.

Alex met Trevin and David just a month after they had started dating. Just one fucking month too late. Alex had fallen in love at first sight, the confident and cocky Trevin Mendoza alpha male to Alex's outrageous ingenue. Alex was a performer, a dancer in the theater scene, expressing himself in plays and performances. Trevin actually lived it while Alex just mimicked it.

Alex was always acting. Nothing was ever *real*. Someone else's script, or being someone else entirely. Pretending, performing, role-playing. But last night had been a prelude to something else. If Trevin lets him, maybe Alex will finally be brave enough to take off his mask and show the world the truth.

If he lives long enough.

What is that thing in the white? There was a sniffling neek in the corner at the back of the diner whining about Armageddon, convinced by his fellow outcasts on unsociable media that the thing in the white is some monster from the future. Alex's mother used to read him a bedtime story when he was young about a little boy who dressed like a bear. The boy in the story put on a furry costume every day to be fierce and brave. Alex became a performer because he wanted to be something else. Whatever was in the white was just something normal dressed like a big, bad bear.

There are a dozen people in the line, batshit crazy to be out in this blizzard. Alex couldn't see five feet in any direction, but he only needed to see Trevin, and Trevin was never more than an arm's length away. The people in the lead are from this town and seem to know when to turn right or left down anonymous streets lined with buildings that are usually hidden by overwhelming white. The church is only three blocks away, but the trek feels like three miles in the snow.

Zack is right in front of Trevin. Alex might have been jealous of how close Trevin keeps the fat kid, but Zack is not Trev's type. At all. Maybe Trev just needs him because the kid is local and he knows the town better than a couple of tourists. "…*a couple…*" Alex smirks. The words sound perfect in his head.

Something bright. In the white. Like a star shining through a thick fog, finally resolving into the letter "t." Alex realizes it is a cross. Rising. Floating. Into the white above them. What did the mayor of this goddamned town call it? The Church of Ascension. How appropriate.

The light becomes diluted as the wind comes up and erases everything else around them, then returns as just a faint glowing smudge, getting higher and smaller, until it disappears.

They are too late.

Trev shoves Zack behind a vehicle mostly buried beside them. Trev is strong and sure, decisive and dashing. He does not even look back to see if Alex follows him behind the car; he knows wherever he goes, Alex will be right behind.

The snow almost entirely covers the Buick in front of them. Zack looks like a furry pig trying to burrow itself into a snowbank. Trev is on hand and knees, peering around the bumper to try and see. Alex looks with him, his face close enough to smell the masculine scent of Trevin even over the whipping wind.

The strong gusts subside a moment, as if blocked by some great windbreak. Alex watches over Trevin's shoulder as the church is systematically dismantled. People flee the structure as walls peel away and the interior is swept up like someone picking apart a gingerbread house. The sound of destruction should be a roar, but instead, it is a muffled effect, like someone has turned the volume way down on a scene being played back on a television screen.

The little Asian spitfire from the diner runs *toward* the church instead of away. She stands nearly as high as Alex's pierced nipples, yet she forges into danger against the tide of terrified people. The white makes everything seem more mirage than a real disaster, as if the people that disappear are figments of imagination rather than flesh and blood.

A rhyme from Sunday school wells in Alex's mind, his hands pressed together and head bowed: *Here's the church; here's the steeple. Open them up, see all the people? Close it up while they pray. Open them up, they all went away.*

The white claims one here, another there, screaming in a descending volume until it is nothing. Either the last sound is swallowed by the snow or swallowed by something else.

Alex ducks down, huddling behind the car.

"We're going to die," Zack mumbles.

"Shut up," Trevin commands. "Stay low. The fools running out in the open are easier targets."

But maybe Zack is right. Maybe this is it. Last night had been magical. A fairy tale. Perhaps the fates had let them have their happy ending for a reason. Maybe their ever after will only be a few hours long.

Alex has wanted this for so long he does not even know how to put it into words. Even last night, the purpose behind his passion had never been said aloud. He has to tell Trevin. He has to tell him how he feels.

"Trev, listen, last night—"

"I don't want to talk about last night, Alex. People are dying all around us. And David could be anywhere. He could be right here."

"It's not just about last night. It's been about the last few years. I want you to know how I—"

"Not now," Trevin cuts him off. "Let's talk about it tomorrow."

But what if there is no tomorrow? What if this is it? The present. A present that for so long Alex had thought he would never be able to unwrap. But here they are. They had made it to the end, still together. David is done. Alex is Trevin's tomorrow.

So if Trevin wants to wait one more day, Alex can push it off 'til tomorrow. Again. What is one more tomorrow after so many?

Then Trevin's eyes widen. Zack opens his mouth to scream, but no sound comes out. They are both looking behind Alex.

He is plucked. Like a pink flower. Damn his flamboyant hair, it had probably drawn unwanted attention. Whatever the thing in the white, it was just something dressed as a bear. A fucking polar bear. It carries him up as gently and quickly as a gust of wind. He is covered neck to toe in ski gear, but he has the sensation of fur or wool under his thick gloves.

Like floating away, carried up by helium balloons.

Alex screams. Louder than when one of his piercings had gotten ripped out during a dance routine in a performance of *Cats* three summers ago. Louder than when he had seen his mother hit by a bus right before his very eyes. Louder than when he'd been cast as the lead in *Fiddler*. He screams and screams and screams.

The thing in the polar bear parka pauses. Below, *far* below, at the edge of the white, Alex watches as the last standing wall of the church is peeled away. For a moment, the detached wall gives the whole scene shelter from the wind. All of the parts, for just a few seconds, become suspended some thirty feet in the sky. Up so high, Alex sees it all.

He sees Trev. Looking up. Their eyes meet, and Alex knows everything is going to be okay. He stops screaming. "I love you," he cries out, sure the wind carries his words toward Trevin and not away. Then he is lifted higher. The white erases the ground, the group, the church, even Trevin. But Alex does not scream again. Everything is going to be okay. He did not get Trevin just to lose him again.

Or is it too late?

Did he lose his chance the moment his feet left the ground?

Alex is lifted up, up, up. Higher and higher. Like an elevator that rushes all the way to the top floor. How high is he going? Is the white still snow or has it become clouds? White, white, white. Then the wind ceases, the snow stops falling, and something is different. Still white and white and white.

Even inside.

Then black.

-21°

Aspen Wang stands still, churchgoers stampeding all around her through the blizzard. The world is hushed, although the look of terror on the faces of the dozens rushing past suggests there should be a cacophony. The fear in their eyes is of folks in the midst of devastation, avoiding destruction, trying to reconcile reality with annihilation. Yet the world remains muffled, even the wind whispering instead of wailing.

Like watching a scene on the other side of the passing cars of a mile-long train, the white obscures and reveals the events before her in regular intervals. Aspen watches the last section of the exterior wall disappear into the sky. The church's interior is revealed in total, like a scale model of an architect's proposal. Then, like they are chess pieces that have fallen to a better opponent, the last pawns are removed from the board: the altar absconded, the sacristy separated, pews preempted, half the floor ripped away like a Band-Aid.

All around Aspen, the Christians who had holed up in the church disappear into the white. They slip in and out of sight within the blizzard, most of them unprepared for the whipping wind and deadly low temps. Frostbite would get them in mere minutes. In the end, their attire might not matter; some things will kill them faster than the cold. Sometimes she glimpses one running toward her, and then a swirl of snow and they are gone. Others are shadows that pass on her left and right, and many just wink away, like shade eliminated by sudden sunlight. Some are no more than a dozen feet away when they fall *up*, pulled into the sky as though an alien ship is beaming victims into outer space. A few make it past her, surviving long enough to find another shelter. Aspen thinks of her Uncle Bobby, who grew a patchy black beard every winter, a tangled mess that always collected a handful of crumbs at every meal: "I'm saving a little for later." The thing in the white thinks of them all as just crumbs.

What is it?

Someone at the diner suggested it was something from the future. They'd seen the reports online. A tear in reality let through a monster from some terrible tomorrow. Roman did not believe it, so Aspen discounted it. Time travel was not the likeliest answer anyway. Mad science. Errant experiment. Gamma mutation. Genetic mistake. Maybe even some prehistoric anomaly. Certainly not some creature from the twenty-second century...

And then suddenly Aspen stands alone. The ubiquitous white is suffocating. Every exhale adds to the white, as if her own breath is contributing to her erasure. Maybe that is what it really is. Reality unraveling, the world unmaking itself. Her mother was never a religious woman, but she had always told Aspen that she had to find her own way. Aspen had gone to Sunday school with her cousin Lani, and they had learned how God made the world. Aspen still remembers memorizing the first passages of Genesis: "In the beginning, God created the heaven and the earth. And the earth was without form, and void..." Perhaps God is erasing His work. Maybe He is taking it back. All around Aspen is void. The great unmaking.

Maybe the thing in the white is like Jonah's whale, swallowing the world one by one.

She looks up to the heavens. *Am I next?* she wonders. The white gives no answers. She knows she should move; she knows it won't matter if the monster comes for her; she cannot take a step. Something had propelled her toward the church when she saw it being dismantled, sure her mother was inside. Now fear has paralyzed her, stopped her cold in the wide open, ripe for rapture if the thing in the white determines she is next.

Nothing. Nothing. Nothing.

Somewhere else (direction and distance are tricky in the snowstorm), the terrible, wonderful sound of a sonic boom cracks. The thing that razed the church is gone. Somewhere else. For now. Making noise in the distance. Far enough away that Aspen feels that her time to die is no longer imminent. Just eventual.

Aspen moves.

The church is gone. Everything. Aspen stands near a water pipe sticking out of the ground that indicates the former location of the bathroom. A geyser sprays into the frosty air, wind and cold making ice and fog out of the spray before even a droplet hits the ground, whipped away by sustained gusts. A drainpipe once attached to a toilet is just a hole to nowhere now.

If her mother had been here, she is long gone. Either escaped or absconded with.

Over the mourning moan of wind sucking through this new void between buildings, like a gust through a mountain pass, Aspen can hear something other than the natural dirge. A buzzing sound more aggressive and less solemn. Like angry hornets readying an attack. Something defiant in all this wailing impotence.

Aspen forges ahead into the white. Roman had insisted she take a parka from an old woman who had stayed back at the diner in exchange for looking for the woman's sister at the church. Aspen cinches the hood tight and pulls a scarf over her face so it's just her eyes against the cold wind. Her black bangs are a welcome respite blowing across her eyes as, otherwise, it is only endless alabaster. "...*the earth was without form, and void...*" She shudders. It is cold, and she is alone.

A parsonage sits next to the church, a small home humble in comparison to the opulent place of worship. Aspen had watched as the ornamental interior of the main church structure had been collected and carried away, borne up on something that she either could not see or her mind refused to register. Gold and silver and gems and marble, more ornamentation that the collective decor of the rest of all Zukunft Falls, Aspen suspects. But this small parsonage is just one story, and even in the erasure of white, Aspen can see it end to end standing at the middle of the west wall.

Or what had once been the west wall. It has been shoved aside by whatever thing in the white dismantled the church. The wall had fallen in, not flat, but rather at a 45° incline that would have made a perfect ramp to jump a snowmobile if one had either the machine itself or the capability to see far enough to know where one might land. The roof had fallen in, like a cap tilted down over one's eyes.

Aspen does not want to look, but she does. Beneath her boots, a massive footprint in the snow has compressed the powder beneath her sole into sheer ice. The wind has already started to fill in the impression, obscuring the edges and erasing the true scope of the print. Drifts disguise the extent of the impression, and Aspen considers that a mercy. There are things in this world that are better not to know. The true size of impending doom is better left a mystery.

The buzzing sound is closer, that mechanical hum that reminds Aspen of mowing lawns. Now, lawnmowers seem as far away and long ago as "*In the beginning...*" She moves toward the toppled wall, and the droning sound comes from within. She leans forward, noting the hoarfrost turning the blue siding to dull cobalt. Icicles that recently depended from the roofline are now scattered along the tilted wall, caught in the ridges of the shiplap.

Then a blade of a chainsaw cuts through, the spinning teeth coming right for Aspen's face.

She flinches back as metal bites and gnashes the whirling white.

The chainsaw cuts up and through, four feet higher from the starting point before being retracted. Then it erupts through again, perpendicular, four feet across. Then again, down. Lastly, across, a four foot by four foot square collapsing in.

A wisp of a fellow pops up out of the wall, face smudged with snow and scree. Blood smears his forehead from his black hairline down to his eyebrows, caused by an unseen gash or an absent victim. His first arm out has an icepick duct taped around his forearm. Aspen could not imagine what the ice pick could do against the thing in the white, the monster that made the footprint. Like a wasp irritating a rhino.

Then he flails, his other arm incapacitated, taped to his torso to render it immobile. He looks like a soldier with an improvised field-dress returned to battle one-armed. Aspen reaches out and pulls him up and out of the wreckage, careful to avoid the icepick.

She looks at the guerrilla bandage, efficient and effective. That describes her mother perfectly.

"Who—?" Aspen starts to ask.

Then a woman rises from the square cut in the toppled wall. She has a scarf wrapped around her head like an Arabian princess crossing the Sahara in a sandstorm. Somewhere along the way she appropriated a camouflage jacket in spatters of white and gray. Gloves that look thermodynamic and ergonomic clutch a chainsaw that idles in her right hand. With her left hand, she pulls back the scarf from her face. She looks like a badass out of a post-apocalyptic future, but she is a figure from Aspen's past. The first figure from Aspen's past.

"Mom!"

-22°

Trevin sits in an abandoned car, buried under a snowbank that slopes up the trunk and over the roof. The windshield has a thinner scrim across the glass and could be whisked away by the wiper blades, but Trevin does not reach for the switch. He doesn't want to see what's out there. He refuses to turn on the headlights because it will only illuminate the white. There is not enough darkness already without adding any more light to the situation. It is better not to know.

Zack sits in the backseat, riding bitch through the apocalypse. Trevin insisted on leaving the passenger side open in case he sees David run by. If fate would bring them back together, then the future might not seem so dire. Yet Trevin and Zack remain alone.

"Alex...," Zack whispers.

"He's dead," Trevin snaps, and Zack shuts up.

Trevin does not want to talk about Alex. He'd been a problem solved or a solution lost. In either case, he had served a purpose. His ridiculous pink hair must have acted like an eager first-grader in the front row: *pickmepickmepickme*. The thing in the white had chosen. Alex had been swept up into the atmosphere like a helium balloon, and Trevin had been the one to let go of the string. He kept Zack close because he figured the guy would be more tantalizing to a predator, all big and slow and juicy. He had kept Alex close because attention is always drawn to a flame, and Alex Dove positively blazed.

"How do we know it's not coming back?" Zack asks.

"We don't," Trevin says.

"How do we know it won't grab a car as easily as a building or any of those people?"

"We don't."

"Maybe we should move on," Zack suggests. He won't leave on his own. The kid thinks of Trevin as some sort of big brother. Trevin thinks of this guy as a plump alternative to his own scrawny ass. Any hungry monster should always grab the berry instead of the twig.

"Maybe."

Move where, though? Trevin wonders. He would have been moving along a long time ago if he knew a direction. If he had any idea where to find a way out of this town. He had been drunk in the booze bus up from the base of the mountain and had not paid attention to where the town was located or what the road back down the mountain looked like. Trevin has no idea even which direction is up the mountain or down. Zack might know, but he might not. The teenager is scared and self-absorbed, and Trevin would not bet his life that Zack could lead them to safety.

He wouldn't even wait for David anymore. Not after what he saw. Or what he didn't see.

There are things out there that are better left unseen.

The inside of the car is deathly cold. Zack wanted him to start the car, but neither of them knew how to hot-wire a Hyundai. Besides, the back half of the sedan is under six feet of snow. Trevin has seen enough movies to know that they would die of carbon monoxide poisoning with the tailpipe buried under the bank. He is not going to die in a fucking Hyundai.

That's finally what got him moving. If Trevin was going to freeze to death, better on the streets of Zukunft Falls than inside some Korean piece of shit.

"What other places are near the church?" Trevin asks.

Zack leans forward, shifting the car in the snow and causing a muf-fled *flump* of a miniature avalanche off the rear left side.

"Dottie's Bakery. A mini-mart. Domino's."

"Jesus. Anything that doesn't have to do with food?" Trevin snaps.

"But I'm hungry," Zack answers in a whine.

"And if that fucking thing in the white runs out of people poppers, where do you think it is going to be looking for a fix. Same place as you and me, dude." Trevin wants to call him a goddamn idiot, but he needs his decoy until he gets out of this cold, white hell. "Anyplace else?"

"There's a little comic book shop on the corner," Zack says.

Perfect. Trevin's new plan is to find other survivors of this turd-stain town, and hopefully, someone will know how to get the hell down the mountain. Head out of this snow. Get back to civilization. Trevin is going to run all the damn way back to California and live the rest of his life on the beach, by the waves, forever and ever. And there ought to be geeks in a comic book store. And geeks know shit.

"C'mon," Trevin says, opening the door. Zack scurries out after him. Trevin stands in the wind, bracing against the blizzard and staring into the face of nothingness. The world is white. Erased. For a moment, Trevin suspects the world is gone and they are all alone in it. Just two young men and a hungry monster in the white. Then he shakes it away. Motions to his bait. Zack leads, moving with his foot along the curb so as not to get lost in the whiteout. Trevin follows in his footsteps like the fat dude is some sort of human shield.

They come to the intersection, the crossing light above them glow-ing bright in the white. "Walk," but they retreat back to the storefront on the corner. The comic book shop affords terrible protection. The storefront is plate glass, hoarfrost edging the panes like gray shores around a frozen pond. The front door is covered with superheroes, but whatever that thing in the white is, it is no match for Batman or Wonder Woman or even King fuckin' Kong. The soundtrack of an old movie sounds as Trevin and Zack push open the door, unlocked. Trevin recognizes it as he sees the red and blue crest on the chest of a standee greeting shoppers at the front door. It is the *Superman* theme from an old movie.

A half dozen teenage boys who have all surely only seen a naked woman between the pages of magazines sit huddled among hobbits and heroes and avatars of all sorts of anime. And one girl, goth as fuck: black hair, makeup, shoes, clothes, mood. One look and Trevin knows all the boys love her and she is oblivious and uninterested.

"So, what the fuck is that thing out there?" Trevin asks the egg-heads. The teens all have glowing screens in their hands. Surely, the nerds with noses to their smartphones know something. "Tell me the goddamn military is on the way."

"It's the future, dude," answers one. "We are obsolete."

"What the hell does that mean?"

"We broke the world wide open," the goth girl sighs. "Messin' with shit. Trying to fix the future, we brought tomorrow to today. It's all over social media. Crazy-ass, eco-asshole scientists were trying to make something to reverse global warming. They tried to harness the power of absolute zero."

"Conspiracy theory bullshit," Trevin says.

"Not necessarily," disagrees one of the girl's geeky boyfriends. "Absolute zero is the state at which atoms cease movement. Zero degrees on the Kelvin scale. The lowest temperature *theoretically* possible. But what if there is a scale on the opposite side? We have negative degrees Celsius and Fahrenheit. We have degrees below freezing. What if there is negative Kelvin?"

"How can something get colder than *absolute zero*?" Zack asks skeptically.

"Maybe you ought to be asking, 'What happens on the other side of absolute zero?'" the teen with a zillion zits quizzes. "Think about moving forward. Running. Gradually, you start to slow down. After a few moments, you come to a complete stop. The only direction further in reverse is to go backward. Maybe those stilled atomic particles start to reverse. Move back through time. Maybe it also unravels everything we thought we knew about biology and physics."

"You think they made something colder than absolute cold and it broke time? Created that goddamn monster in the white?" Trevin challenges.

"Why the hell not?" the goth girl pushes back. "That thing should be impossible. Creatures from the future should not be tromping around Zukunft Falls. So how else do you explain it? Those idiot geniuses broke the thermometer and it shattered time. It remade the rules of biology. And it made the world *frosty*."

"It sounds like the plot from one of your comic books," Zack says.

"You wouldn't understand, Gurp. You don't *have* a fucking future."

Trevin steps between Zack and the goth teen girl, who is even a bigger dick to the guy than Trev has been. "We need to get out of this town. Any of you nerds have a digital compass or a self-driving snowmobile or a short wave radio that can call for some help?"

"We might be surrounded by comic books, but this isn't a movie," goth girl drones, as if Trevin might be the dumbest creature she has ever laid eyes on. "We don't have spare parts laying around to build a transmitter on the spot, asshole."

"Jeez, Jillian, he's just trying to help," Zack says, defending his new best friend.

"Shut up, Gurp," Jillian commands in stone-cold monotone. "I thought you'd have killed yourself after the über-embarrassing thing with Mandy Ryder and the Frost Festival."

The six nerdy boys titter like tweens.

Zack turns as pink as Alex's hair.

Trevin sneers, "I hope that thing eats the whole lot of you little bitches before you ever see a nak—"

Then the *Superman* theme plays behind him, and Trevin's heart skips a beat. For a moment, he thinks a giant hand is reaching in behind him, ready to snatch him up and take him away. He turns without breathing. It is just the small young woman in the old lady's parka who rushed into the melee back at the church instead of running away.

Trevin smirks as he sees six teenage boys all stare at the subject of many an anime wet dream as young woman pulls back her hood and looks across the gathered group.

Someone follows her in, pulling away a headdress that covers her whole face. The resemblance is undeniable. So the girl had found her mother.

Then someone else is behind the young woman's mother. A lean figure covered head to toe. The last one in pulls down goggles with an arm accessorized with an ice pick, and Trevin would know those eyes anywhere.

David.

-23°

Roman and six townspeople survey the perimeter constructed around Zukunft Falls. The bruiser's name is Butch (of course, it is), and he stares down the wall like he thinks he can find a weak point and knock it down. Mayor Brick's braggadocio finally fizzles as he sees the true scope of the barrier. There's a woman who looks like a panda in black and white, another has red boots brighter than a stoplight, and a third wears an eyepatch and carries a rifle. An older fellow with a mustache wider than his head brings up the rear, carrying a double-barrel shotgun like he means it.

There is silence amongst the group. They are awestruck. This is bigger than any of them can understand.

Even Roman.

Twenty years in the wilderness and Roman has experienced some harrowing encounters with local predators. He had faced down a grizzly protecting her cub a few years back and came away with the coat he is wearing now. He'd been bitten by a rattler some ten years ago and suffered excruciating pain as the venom worked through his system. A mountain lion had attacked him his first spring on the mountain, and the cat had gotten away after a ferocious fight, scars from teeth and claws marking Roman's face and shoulder. The encounters with these predators would be like swatting gnats compared to what he is up against in the white.

The wall stands some twenty feet high. The wind abates momentarily now and again, affording a glimpse of the top of the wall. Constructed of recycled materials from the resort and the school, Roman picks out components like a basketball hoop from the gymnasium, a door with the number 362 from the hotel, luggage, sections of red brick wall and concrete chunks the size of cars, metal beams and thick timbers, whole sections of wall and large swaths of floor, drywall, plaster, ceramic, stone. Occasionally, a vehicle sticks out: an arctic cat with an Enchanted Point Ski Resort logo on the side, a school bus set vertically amongst the wreckage, numerous tourists' trucks with out-of-state plates. It is demolition repurposed as a trap.

They have completed walking the entire eastern perimeter of the town. The debris from the resort and the school alone is not enough to surround the whole town with a twenty-foot wall, but escaping west up the mountain and doubling back along the wall to get to lower elevations comes with its own dangers. If the wall is meant to corral the citizens of the Falls, then the thing in the white will be patrolling its length.

Roman pauses. It has been twenty minutes since the last blast of baritone thunder. They heard the last sonic boom over the argument between Butch and Mayor Brick about going around the wall or going over. They were warming up in a small gas station owned by the woman who is dressed like a panda. They had to stop and warm up regularly. The rest of them have modern attire, heat packs, space-age material, layers and layers, yet they cannot stand the cold longer than fifteen minutes. Roman is covered in dead furs and feathered garments and could spend all night out in the cold.

Roman is certain the pause was due to the church being dismantled. Someone's misfortune was their opportunity. He hopes Aspen's group made it to the church in time to warn the parishioners. How long does the demolition take? The thing in the white is efficient and expedient. It might return at any time.

"Time's up," Roman says over the whistling wind. "We need to get back."

"Then we climb over," Mayor Brick concedes, staring up. "Like Butch suggested."

Twenty feet. Difficult climb. Ten minutes for someone of average physical ability? By the looks of the townsfolk, just Butch with the bad attitude might make it up and over in that amount of time. The rest would take longer, maybe never even make it. And that is without being plucked from the perimeter like dandruff off a collar.

Roman shakes his head. "Suicide."

"Staying here is suicide," Mayor Brick says.

Roman looks into the white. Is it here? Is it looking back?

He feels like he is being hunted.

"I can make it over," Butch brags, grabbing a bumper of a Buick from Jersey. He lifts himself, making a chin-up look easy.

"I need to get out of here, too," declares the puffy panda. She is fifty pounds overweight and unsuited to scale a twenty-foot barrier.

"It will be back," Roman warns, looking over his shoulder into the inscrutable screen of snow. "It may already be."

The portly panda finds some stairs recycled from the resort that crouches askew on the wall of wreckage. She has hauled herself up four feet already, an impressive feat, and looks back. "All the more reason to get the fuck out of this tow—" She goes up and up, past where Butch has managed half the height of the wall already, higher than the twenty feet, her feet disappearing into the white as she ascends. She does not even scream. The woman is either in shock or already dead.

"My God," whispers the woman closest to Roman, and she sprints into the white. Then Roman sees her red boots, like a flare fired into the sky, up and up and up. She does not go as quietly as the last victim: "Gaaaaaaaa—!"

The school bus is wedged into the wall in such a way that the back emergency doors face down, six feet off the ground. The woman with the eyepatch and the mustachioed old man point their weapons at the white as Roman yanks open the back hatch on the bus.

"In," Roman hisses at the Mayor, frozen in fear and staring into the snow.

"We need to run," he argues.

The man with the shotgun and the incredible mustache agrees, charging into the whiteout like a colonial soldier running into combat, and then a less colloquial battle cry: "Motherfu—" The shotgun sounds, a flash of gunpowder sparking the white a little brighter. The blast occurs some thirty feet in the air, higher than the wall.

"We need to get inside the bus," Roman tells the Mayor.

Mayor Brick nods.

Roman boosts the big bastard up and in. The politician is flabby and doughy. He hardly makes it easy. Then the woman with the eye-patch. She is light, and Roman can almost throw her up and in. Then he looks up at Butch, three-quarters of the way up the wall already.

"Jump down, Butch," Roman calls out, his voice just loud enough to carry over the wail of the wind. All he can see is Butch's expensive hiking boots.

"Fuck you, Mountain Ma—"

Then Butch is gone.

Roman grabs the edge of each side of the emergency door and lifts himself up and in. The Mayor and the woman with the eyepatch sit on the backs of the school bus seats, the whole vehicle set with the windshield pointing up. Roman stands with one leg straddling each side of the emergency exit. He imagines some monstrous paw coming up through the open double doors and snagging a leg. The wind obscures even the six feet between the doorway and the ground. Roman stares into the white.

Whitewhitewhitewhite.

He is sure the thing in the white will not destabilize the wall by plucking three little morsels out of the school bus. It will not endanger the structure. Not yet. The trap is to keep everyone inside. There are still hundreds of people corralled inside Zukunft Falls. The predator does not have to compromise its wonderful wall to get at three minor snacks.

They wait. And wait. Minutes pass. Nothing.

Then, in the distance, the baritone blast. It is safe to escape.

Roman drops down, helps the woman out, and they both lower the mayor to the snowy ground.

"Let's get back to the diner," Roman says.

"Wait," Mayor Brick says. He stares into the white, along the wall. The wind abates a moment, and Roman sees it. A cross. From the church.

The mayor moves forward. The woman in the eyepatch wants to see, too. Roman follows. After the debris of the church, the wall ends. This is where the construction stops. Beyond, there is white. Facing almost due north, they could exit, turn right, and head down the mountain.

"We can run for it," Mayor Brick states. "That thunder sounded all the way across town."

"With the white and the wind, you cannot be sure where the mon—"

Then it sounds off again, surely distant. It is almost too far to hear over the moaning wind. The mayor ignores Roman and steps around the end of the wall. The woman follows him, rifle at the ready. Roman stands by the remnants of tangled oak pews. Mayor Brick and his armed escort disappear into the white.

The baritone blast goes off again, faint, just as far.

Then a rifle shot and the woman's voice, a screaming wail: "What white devil is th—"

Roman stares into the white. Watching. Waiting. What? White and white and white and...

Mayor Brick comes running toward Roman, his face as white as the snow, his eyes as wide as his gaping mouth, screaming in horror. He is running faster than anyone would ever believe he was capable. But not fast enough. Fifteen feet from Roman and the edge of the wall, he stops suddenly, as if he has hit an invisible wall. He looks at Roman for a split second, scream stuttering.

"There's anoth—"

Then Mayor Brick disappears into the white.

Roman turns, climbing into a crevasse between the altar and the metal wall that had once made a stall in the church's public restroom. Someone has taped an announcement to the beige surface advertising a bake sale on Tuesday. All proceeds will go to the church renovation project. Roman whispers darkly, "I hope that bake sale brings in about a million bucks, cuz the church needs to be rebuilt from the ground up."

He waits. And waits. Minutes pass. Nothing.

But Roman Carver doesn't move. For the first time since he left civilization behind and embraced the wild, the wild is too much for him. He had almost died by bear, by lion, by snake, yet this is the first time in twenty years that Roman is truly terrified.

The mayor's last words echo in his head.

There's another.

There are *two* things out there in the white.

-24°

Rhonda had never had children of her own. If she had ever wanted to, it was too late by the time the thought had occurred to her. Her twenties were a blur, one relationship after another. She had hit her stride in her thirties, finding power in the attraction of men and using them up like people did cell phones nowadays, tossing them aside when a new and improved model came along. She'd been nearing forty before she paused to acknowledge the passing of time. She could still captivate anyone with a wandering eye, even frat boys with the stamina to keep up with her, but she had started to feel the tug of something she might have missed.

It had been momentary regret. The man-train kept chugging, and when the passengers had started to thin out, the prime baby-bearing years were already behind her. If she had wanted to start a family, she would have had to end her ambivalent lifestyle.

Then fifty loomed.

Fifty, tomorrow.

Tomorrow?

She huddles in an alleyway behind a dumpster like a homeless person who has taken too many wrong turns in life. It is so...damned... cold... Cradled in her arms is the closest thing to a baby that she has ever had in her long life. Esther is tucked into her jacket, the old woman nearly frozen to the bone. She is still shivering, so that is good. Rhonda knows enough that when the shivering stops, things get deadly. Hypothermia will set in. They must be on the edge of such dire degrees now. The temperature outside is deadly, but the only direction she can go is back out into the white.

And she can't.

Rhonda can't do it.

It is the alabaster apocalypse. The white end of days. Icy Armageddon. And Rhonda has had enough.

She had joined the crew heading out to warn the churchgoers about getting the hell out of the holy house before Satan's giant spawn wrecked the place, but they had arrived too late. What had she seen? What had she fucking *seen*? Rhonda could not even consider it. What she thought she saw was impossible.

She had run. She had come all that way to find Esther, but when she had seen what she had seen, she'd run the other way.

Rhonda had stumbled through the white away from the church. The others she had found at the diner scattered in every direction. She'd seen the small young Asian woman in the old lady's parka defy the tide of escapees, actually running *toward* the church. She'd been looking for her missing mother. Esther is not Rhonda's mother, so Rhonda had run away. Shadows had been moving around her, and she'd stifled a scream at everyone, so terrified that it was a part of that thing she had seen in the white. But it had just been cars, mostly buried, or buildings, still and still standing, or a signpost that might have indicated a school crossing (no more school) or no parking (the streets are impassable anyway) or a stop sign where everyone ran right by. The only sign that should be showing is, "The end is nigh."

"The end is fucking white," Rhonda says to herself now, as she huddles in an alleyway, slowly dying.

Then, as she fled, scared and irrational, a pair of shadows had taken shape into people. She had followed them into a bakery set adjacent to a funny book shop. Inside, a dozen people had been huddled. Rhonda had not recognize any of them, yet they had all looked the same. Horror had made them all look alike.

One of the people she had followed inside wore a black robe, like a pastor.

"Are you from the church?" Rhonda had asked.

The pastor had been afraid to even speak; she just nodded.

"Did you see an old woman there? Maybe a little confused? Like she didn't know what was going on."

"Do any of us know what is going on?" the pastor whispered.

Rhonda had never had much patience for God, let alone His flock. "You know damn well what I mean. Did you see her?"

The pastor had nodded again.

Rhonda had looked at the door of the bakery. It had been warm in there. Not white. Somewhere far away, she had heard that baritone bellow of thunder that suggested the thing in the blizzard was somewhere farther away. "Goddamn," she had said, unconcerned with the pastor next to her and her pious shit.

So Rhonda had gone back out to look for Esther. She had found the old woman in a snowbank in the alleyway half a block away, curled into a ball. Rhonda had worried that she might be too late, but as she unzipped her thermal jacket and pulled the old woman against her, Esther had responded, hugging close. A good sign.

She has not heard the thunderous bass in many minutes. The silence suggests danger might be close. So she sits with Esther in the alleyway, minutes passing as the temperature drops and drops and drops. She might have staved off hypothermia for Esther for a while, but not forever. Could she drag the old woman to safety? They need to get somewhere warm. If the white won't get them, the cold will.

"Esther?" Rhonda says, and the woman stirs against her. "We need to find shelter." Esther nods feebly. "Can you walk?" Esther pulls away, getting to her feet with no more steadiness than Bambi on the ice.

Rhonda takes the old woman by the hand and leads her out to the mouth of the alley. She pauses. The wind whips by, the white a turbulent screen that obscures everything beyond a few feet. There might not be a street to see, or a town beyond, or a world where anything made sense anymore.

"It's alright, dear," Esther says, a weak voice but strong enough to carry over the whistling wind. "I'm used to not knowing where I am going. If you're not sure, you just fake it until you find something familiar."

Something familiar. Rhonda knows the bakery is warm. The bakery is close. Full circle. Rhonda is always walking in circles through the white. So she moves along the way she had come just a while ago, her steps already obliterated, the fact that she had been here once before already erased. Esther stumbles and falls into the snow. She struggles in the powder, then goes limp. She doesn't have the strength to get back up. The bakery is just around the corner, but it is too far.

Rhonda hooks her arms under Esther's armpits and drags the woman up to the door of the small store on the corner. If the door is locked, Rhonda will have to decide if she will leave the old woman or try to pull her through the snow all the way to the bakery. Neither one of them will make it to tomorrow. But could she live with herself if she left Esther behind? The door isn't locked. It's open. So she drags Esther into the comic book shop.

-25°

Zack sits in the corner of the small store, feeling awkward. He knows all the locals, and all the locals know him as the Gurp. The only one who calls him Zack is Trevin. Now Trevin is reunited with his fiancé. They've been cozy ever since they had found each other, Zack all but forgotten. *All But Forgotten* would be the name of his autobiography if he thought anyone would read it. Hell, no one had probably even read his suicide note currently available online, posted as soon as his smashed phone found a cell signal, and that short story is only sixteen words long.

His whole life summed up in fewer words than years he has lived.

It could be worse, he used to think, when the Gurp nickname was still new and a novelty. His cousin knew a kid in Colorado who burped and farted at the same time. They called him "Two-tones" ever after. They would have called Zack "the Furp."

After an hour of canoodling, Trevin and David wander over to where Zack sits sipping a cup of hot cocoa he made in the microwave next to the inflatable Godzilla figure.

"Trevin tells me you were instrumental in helping him find his way through town," David says.

Zack shrugs.

"Well, thanks for keeping my baby safe."

Zack shrugs again. "I didn't do much." Why was Trevin bragging him up?

"Since you're from around here, do you have any special insight into what's going on out there?"

Zack nods toward the group of sniggering teens behind a display counter with superhero relics. "They say the truth is all over online. It is some kind of creature from the future."

"We ran into your deputy. He said the same thing. He told Doc and me that the military can't even stop it," David says. "But do you believe that?"

Zack shrugs. Why the hell does this guy care what Zack thinks? "That's what they're saying."

"But the future? That's just crazy."

"Jillian says they found something they called a breach. A breach in time. Something tore a hole in reality, and this thing is what came through."

David shakes his head like he can't bear to face the truth.

"Well, it certainly isn't a fucking polar bear," Trevin says.

"They make it seem like some supersized Sasquatch," David says. "That sounds like internet conspiracy."

Zack looks at the group of teens with phones in their hands. They are all connected to something bigger, the world outside this damn doomed town. "I suppose whatever it really is would seem farfetched even if it stepped out of the white and showed itself."

"Did you see it?" David asks.

Zack had seen Alex being carried up into the white. Something big. Something impossible. Zack hadn't been able to look at it too long without feeling like he was going crazy. It certainly could have been the future.

Zack nods. "We saw enough of it."

Zack has never had the opportunity for public displays of affection, so when people are hugging and kissing in front of him, he always feels uncomfortable. He tries to look anywhere but at the two affectionate men that share his corner of the cramped comic book shop.

"We? You and Trev? Or was there someone else with you?" David quizzes.

Trevin's expression is cold and unrevealing.

"What do you mean?" Trevin inquires.

"What happened to Alex?" David asks.

A reaction crosses Trevin's face so quickly that Zack only notices because he expects it. There was something between Trevin and Alex, something that makes Zack squirm a little when he thinks about it. Something Trevin doesn't want David to know about.

"The Hestra mittens," David explains. "Those are the ones he bought on Ventura Boulevard before we left L.A. The only way Alex would part with those mittens is over his dead body. If you have them, then that must mean he didn't make it."

Trevin is speechless. Zack assumes that is a rare thing. "He was taken by the white," Zack finally answers.

David nods. "I'm glad he wasn't alone. I checked his room after all the lights went out and it looked like he didn't make it back last night. I figured he hooked up with some guy for the night. I started toward your room in the south wing. We should have never agreed to separate rooms before the wedding, Trev. What about us is traditional anyway? But then… Everything just went white. The whole world came crashing down. I was hurt, and the Doc saved me. We came looking for you."

Trevin takes David's hands and squeezes. "You found me."

"What about Marilee and Steve and Connie?"

Trevin shrugs. "They were down the other side of the south wing, second floor. There was nothing left of that section of the resort."

David looks away, toward the plate window and the white beyond. They are probably dead. "Anything's possible, though," David says instead.

Zack senses awkwardness, and he always believes he is the cause. "I'm gonna check with everyone else. Maybe someone has a plan."

Jillian McReady glares at Zack as he passes by like this whole blizzard and the monster within it are all the Gurp's fault. Six boys surround her, all elbowing each other to get a position closest to her, so if she decides that this is the end of the world and she settles for last-minute sex with one of the nerds, they each want to be first in line. Zack doesn't even slow down, passing them and heading toward the cute Asian spitfire.

"You found your mom," Zack says.

"A better observation than when you said we are being rampaged by a giant mutated lizard," Aspen quips, not rude but not friendly.

Zack looks at the mom, a hellfire in her eyes and a bump on her head that looks like an almond egg. Worry and relief war across her expression. She has found her daughter, but what horrors await them before they are truly safe? Zack wonders about his own mother, lost somewhere out there.

"Aspen," the mother scolds, stern but gentle. He sees where the daughter gets her talent for duality. Besides Trevin and David, the kids from school, a black woman about the age of his mother, and an old woman who has flesh the color of hoarfrost, these two were the only other people with Zack in the shop. "Maybe not everyone is so lucky. What about your parents, young man?"

Zack shrugs. He refuses to cry in front of the pretty young lady.

Aspen's mother puts a hand on Zack's shoulder, and it is so loving and perfect that he almost breaks down like a blubbering *girl*. "What's your name?"

"Zakaria. Most people call me Zack."

"Most people call you the Gurp," Jillian sneers from halfway across the room.

Then Aspen and her mom both give Jillian the most withering glare ever created. It might have been the sweetest moment of Zack's life if it was not topped a split second later when the black woman smacks Jillian upside the back of the head as she walks by and says, "You watch your nasty little mouth, girl, or next time my hand will be across your face." Six nerds with skinnier chests than even Jillian try to puff up and one even opens his mouth to say something. "I will slap the ever-lovin' balls off of any one of you that makes a peep. You might all be scared out of your minds like I am, but you will keep your ugly words locked up and shit yourselves in peace."

The old woman shuffles slowly behind Zack's ebony angel. Even the glacial grandma gives the group of teens a don't-fuck-with-me glare. They stop in front of Aspen's mom.

"Rhonda Phelps," the black woman says, holding out her hand. "And this is Esther Williams."

Aspen's mom took the hand and shook it. "Doctor Xueman Wang. And this is my daughter, Aspen."

"I've seen your daughter in action," Rhonda says. "She ran right into the white even as the rest of us turned tail."

"I had to find my mother," Aspen answers shyly. "I knew she would be looking for me."

"Feeling better?" Dr. Wang asks the old woman.

Esther twiddles knobbed fingers. "I can't feel the small ones. Or the tips of some others."

"Frostbite," Dr. Wang says. "We need a clinic as soon as possible."

"I'll be fine in the meantime," Esther says.

"Do we know what's next?" Dr. Wang asks. "We can't stay here forever."

"There's a guy named Roman," Rhonda explains. "He went to scout the perimeter. We are supposed to rendezvous back at the diner."

"Roman saved my life," Aspen says.

Zack wishes he could have saved her life. Maybe Aspen would have said his name the way she says Roman's.

"Then it seems I need to meet this guy," Dr. Wang says. She looks across the room at Trevin and David. "Ready to get the hell out of here?"

David nods.

"How about you lot?" Rhonda asks the teens flanked by cardboard cutout heroes saving the world from monsters and aliens. Zack thinks, *That used to be fiction just a few hours ago.*

Jillian waves her phone. "They say the breach is still open. There might be more of those monsters coming through."

"From the future," Dr. Wang says doubtfully.

"Look, lady, comic books have been warning about this kind of shit for forever," Jillian defends. "Climate change. Time travel. Frosty leviathans. It's all real, bitch."

Dr. Wang glares. Zack wonders if the Hippocratic Oath precludes smacking around a belligerent teen?

"Wouldn't you rather take your chances out there than in here?" David asks.

Jillian shakes her head defiantly, rebel to the end. And the boys won't go anywhere without her.

"What about you, Zack?" Dr. Wang asks. "Are you with us, or you want to stay here with them?"

Zack was ready to die this morning. His suicide note is floating out there in the future. He cannot take that back. But he can take it forward. He can look to tomorrow since he might have one now.

Or he might still die a horrible death.

Trevin and David approach. Trevin punches him playfully on the arm. Like a brother. "He's coming with us. Right, Zack?"

And Zack nods.

-26°

Roman manages to crawl to a BMW that probably cost more than anyone in Zukunft Falls made in an entire year, now smashed and worthless, its owner likely a small snack for whatever that thing is in the white.

Things.

"The monsters are smarter than we are," Roman says to no one.

His breath frosts the spiderwebbed glass of the windshield. The temperature is still dropping. With the windchill, it is as cold as Roman has ever experienced. And it is getting colder.

Yet he does not move.

He has developed many different traps in his twenty years in the mountains. Clever. Efficient. Easy. But the monster's plan is ingenious. One thing in the white constructs a barricade, herding the trapped food inside the borders. Like a corral with one exit, and the second predator waits at the gate. Food is delivered like people are pizza. The thing outside the wall also patrols the perimeter, plucking off and eating anyone who tries to climb up and over the barricade.

There is no way out.

There is no way out for *everyone.*

Roman scratches the frost away from the glass and peers through.

White and white and more white. There might be anything out there, or nothing. The other survivors are going to meet him at the diner. Roman has to get back. He has to move forward.

Nothing. Nothing. Nothing.

He opens the door.

Nothing reaches in.

Roman steps out onto the hood of a rusted-out Toyota pickup. He climbs down what were once stairs in the church. He steps into the snow piled at the base of the wall and listens. The wind hums, like a harmonica playing a dirge. Like a siren wailing in the distance, warning against danger. Waaaaaaaatttch owwwwwwwwwwtt! Beeeeeeeeeee caaaaaaaarrrrrrefulllllll!

Bear. Snake. Lion. Roman survived them all.

He has never been so scared.

He steps into the white, forward, onward. He draws the hunting knife that had once saved him from a grizzly. It would do nothing against the thing in the white. But if he had to, it could be used on himself. He does not want to be alive when the thing puts him in its mouth.

Another step. The snow crunches. The ice snaps.

Roman has not heard the blast of baritone that signals that the thing in the white is elsewhere. So close to the border with the second thing on the perimeter, it probably doesn't matter. He cannot fully fathom the true scope of the monster's size, but certainly, if it wants to reach over a twenty-foot wall and pluck him like a flower, then Roman is a rose.

Something moves in the white, and Roman reacts by instinct. Two decades in the wild, he likes to think he has communed with nature to the extent that he is as much animal as man. He can be feral. There was a night a few years ago when he'd been hunting by the light of a full moon, and after he'd slain his prey, Roman had thrown his head back and howled like a wolf. He looks more bear than man. His reflexes are trustworthy, and after he throws himself to the left, something large and white moves through the place where he'd been standing.

Roman runs. He is an animal, and his instinct for flight has kicked in. But panic never fully takes over. He runs with his arms raised, logic still retaining a foothold.

His boots hit the snowy ground, making a muffled thump with each footfall: *flump flump flump flu—*

The ground is gone.

Up. Up. Up. Like Jessica Lange in the hand of Kong, he is lifted higher and higher into the sky. He glimpses the top of the wall as he clears twenty feet in altitude. So it is the monster from the outside of the wall. He was right: it can easily reach over and and grab anything this side of the wall.

Through the static of white and the fog of snow, he sees strands of something like short fur blowing in the wind. It has him in a pincher that reminds him of a crab, but there is flesh beneath the fur, as cold as the arctic air. How can something so cold be so big and so alive? It went against nature. Against physics as Roman knew it. This monster ought to be dead.

At the diner, they had said it came from the future. Wasn't that why he'd left Texas, to get away from the technology and progress? Now here he is, clutched in the cold hand of something evilly evolved. But Roman does not believe in science fiction. He doesn't subscribe to terrible tomorrows. Today is terrifying enough. Wherever, *when*ever, it came from, it is here, and Roman must now face it, so God damn the future.

Up and up and up.

He had raised his arms when he was running so that if he was grabbed like the rest of his party, the thing in the white would not pin his arms at his side. His hands are free, and the knife is still in his fist. He stabs down with the hunting knife, but fur and frigid flesh serve as a natural armor. The blade skitters off the surface of the monster's fist like a penknife across a block of ice, causing no casualty. The thing does not so much as flinch or pause. It brings Roman higher and higher. If he meets a mouth, Roman plans on turning the knife around and plunging the blade into his brain.

But not yet. Roman brings the blade about, pushing the point into the crick of the pincher at the joint. Then he uses his other hand to pound the end of the hilt, like a hammer driving a nail. This succeeds in puncturing the flesh. Like driving a spike into the surface of a frozen pond. Again. Again. His knife buries halfway to the hilt. The thing in the white does not seem to even notice.

Roman pulls the knife out, concerned that a gaping mouth might appear while his blade is incapacitated and he would be eaten alive after all. Pulling the knife free, liquid spurts from the hard flesh. The liquid has a sweet smell that reminds Roman of antifreeze. The color is neon pink and looks like diluted blood on his bearskin coat.

The mouth will be coming at any moment. This all happens in a split second. The sounds of screaming from the others after they'd been plucked lasted only briefly. Roman turns the knife on himself. He does not have enough time to try another assault. He has failed. Now it is time to die.

UpUpUp.

And then down.

The monster drops him. Suddenly Roman is sailing through the white, the wind blowing the snow as gravity pulls him down through the blizzard. He does not even know which way is up or down. How high was he? How hard is he going to hit the ground? Death by blunt force trauma instead of being chewed like a human wad of bubblegum. Better.

Then he hits, glancing the top of the wall, a tangle of furniture cushioning the blow. Roman rolls off to the right and slides down the inside of the barricade, past a demolished snowmobile and a bathtub cracked in half. The bumper of a Buick nails him in the thigh, pain erupting through his brain. But he does not cry out. He keeps falling, silently. Then a piece of rebar sticking out of the wall pierces his right side and Roman groans, biting back a scream. Like a fish on a hook, it holds him.

He is not dead, though.

If he pulls away from the rebar, he might bleed out before he can get back to civilization. As he considers staying or going, he sees why the thing in the white let him go. He has landed right next to the opening in the wall, and three dozen people are trying to rush through the gap. The thing in the white snatches them away one by one. Why settle for a single morsel when the thing can enjoy a smorgasbord?

Roman grabs the end of the rebar and pulls. It yanks free. With two feet of an iron rod sticking out of his side, Roman runs. While the ones trying to escape all think they may be the lucky ones who make it through, Roman races the other way. He knows there is no chance any of them will survive.

-27°

The diner is empty when they return. They are tied together with a long length of rope that Xueman discovered in a maintenance room at the back of the funny book shop. The white at times could erase the person before or behind you even if they were only a half pace away. If anyone took a wrong turn on the journey from the shop to the diner, it could turn out deadly in this weather. Esther had tied a Highwayman's Hitch around each of their forearms, although when Xueman asked where she had learned to tie it, the old woman looked like she didn't understand English. The knot would allow for quick release in case the thing in the white plucked one of them away…

"Not a soul," Rhonda reports after a quick look in the kitchen.

"Where would they go?" Zack asks.

"It looks like they panicked," Rhonda answers. "They must have went off on their own."

"Roman should've been back by now," Aspen tells her mother. There is worry in her voice.

Aspen never had a father figure. Xueman wonders if the girl is fixating too much on the man who had saved her from certain death. A Samaritan is fine, but a savior is dangerous. No man can live up to such expectations. Aspen would end up being disappointed.

"Maybe he didn't make it," Zack offers.

Aspen glares at him but holds her tongue. Xueman knows the only reason the kid did not get stinging words with that sharp look is because Xueman would have scolded Aspen for being too harsh.

"Almost," comes an answer borne on a blast of frigid wind.

A man who looks more savage than savior stumbles through the diner's door. He clutches a two-foot piece of metal rod sticking out the side of his abdomen. Xueman had done her residency in emergency medicine, and she suddenly has a flashback to a woman who'd been brought in after an odd barroom accident, drunk out of her mind with a pool cue sticking all the way through her thigh.

"Help me get him on a table," Xueman barks. Trevin and Rhonda rush to the stumbling man. "Get me some bottled water," she commands Aspen. "And some clean cloth towels," she tells Esther. "I need some light here," she calls to David.

Trevin and Rhonda manage to get Roman to the nearest table. Zack pushes a napkin holder and salt and pepper shakers and a catsup bottle off the surface, all clattering dramatically to the floor. It takes all four of them to get the bulky man on top of the table.

David, with his one good arm, is back with a powerful flashlight. He shines the light on the puncture site, the beam steady enough considering the gagging sounds he is making behind Xueman. The steel section of rebar needs to come out. Based on the angle of penetration, there's a possibility of a punctured liver or intestine or even a kidney. There is no way she can perform surgery in this environment without any medical tools. If something vital is punctured, Roman will die.

Xueman grabs hold of the rod. She looks the wild man in the eyes, the gaze of a wounded animal at the very edge of going feral. "This is gonna hurt," she says.

"I can take i—" And brave sentiment descends into piercing screams as Xueman yanks out the rebar.

Xueman pulls layers of clothes from Roman's torso; they reek like nothing she has ever smelled before. His sleeve is drenched in something pink that smells like sweet juice. His shirt is made of wool, itchy and almost as coarse as the chest hair revealed under all the layers of homemade clothes. The hole in his side is bleeding profusely.

"Water," she demands, reaching back. She did not notice Aspen return, but she has full confidence that her daughter is back and ready. A bottle of water is placed in her hand. Xueman carefully cleans the perimeter of the wound. Gastrointestinal perforation would lead to peritonitis or sepsis. The bleeding looks clean, no contamination from bile or food or stool to indicate an intestinal injury. Xueman assesses that the rebar has punctured the liver.

"Towels," Xueman calls. Someone places them in her hand. She folds them, pressing them over Roman's injury and pushing gently. The first handful soaks quickly. The second almost as fast. But soon the bleeding abates to a slow flow. "Try not to move," she tells Roman, but he has already passed out.

"Will he be okay?" Aspen asks, tears rolling down her face.

"He'll survive getting stabbed..." Xueman answers.

That does not mean he won't get an infection that she does not have an antibiotic for. Or that if they need to run across the rest of Zukunft Falls or even all the way down Bailey's Peak that he won't bleed out before they find a hospital. Or that Roman might be so weak and slow that whatever is in the white will easily pick him off like wounded game.

"...but his chances are fifty/fifty," Xueman tells her daughter.

Xueman has never lied to Aspen. She had told her daughter that her father wanted nothing to do with them and disappeared before she'd even been born. She had never lied about Santa or the Easter Bunny. When Aspen lost a tooth, Xueman had given her ten bucks and took her shopping. At eight, Aspen had asked where babies came from, and Xueman had pulled out a medical journal on reproduction, and they'd spent an afternoon on the science behind it. Xueman's mother had died ten years ago, and Aspen had wondered aloud if she was in Heaven. To which Xueman had replied, "There is no evidence of an afterlife. Anecdotal experience suggests a biological function of brain decay, where a bright light at the end of a tunnel merely represents the final burst of dying cells. Life is energy, Aspen, and now *lǎolao* is returned to the entropy of the universe."

She has never lied, and she is not going to start now.

"Keep pressure on the wound," Xueman tells Trevin. He nods. David stays close, holding the flashlight. Xueman passes Roman off. She needs to get this blood off her hands. She moves to the kitchen to find a sink and realizes, as the adrenaline fades, that she was maybe too harsh with Aspen earlier. Sometimes she can be too blunt with the truth.

She hears someone approach from behind her. "Don't worry too much," Xueman consoles. "His chances aren't much worse than anyone else's."

"That's good," Zack answers, instead of Aspen. "Did you see his eyes? Under the pain? He knows something. He *saw* something."

Xueman looks back as she runs water over her hands and arms up to her elbows, grabbing a bottle of dish soap and squirting unsparingly. Aspen is at Roman's side, repeating encouraging words to the unconscious man. It isn't romantic. It's more dangerous than that. It is the effect of an absent father.

Roman saved Aspen's life. Now Xueman maybe saved his. Even Steven.

Xueman looks at Zack, who maybe knows a thing or two about the look under the pain in someone's eyes. The kid knows something, too. He must have seen that something in his reflection in a mirror on more than one occasion. She noticed the pistol tucked into his overflowing waistband back at the funny book shop. Xueman suspects he was not carrying it for personal protection before the thing in the white attacked.

"You think whatever Roman might have discovered out there in the blizzard is worse than anything we already know? The facts are terrifying enough. A ten-story monster hunting down everyone in this town is about as scary as it gets," Xueman says, drying her hands, looking at the unconscious man on the table. "Right?"

"Maybe he knows the truth," Zack suggests.

The deputy at the bar had believed it was a creature from the future. Something impossible. But Xueman isn't ready for the future. She has her hands full with the now, and her heart full of what is happening right now. She can't consider tomorrow until she survives today. As far as Xueman is concerned, the future can go fuck itself.

"I don't need the truth," Xueman whispers. "I just need to keep Aspen away from it."

Xueman has always been the one with the answers. Ever the cool head that prevailed. When other people lost it in an emergency, Xueman had been steady. Then she'd seen something that she could not comprehend and had passed out cold in a dead faint, logic rebelling to the point of blackout.

For once, Xueman does not want to know.

The kid, either as willfully clueless as the doctor with three PhDs or more clever than he looks, just nods.

-28°

There is something Trevin is not telling him, but David does not know what it is. Something about Alex. Is Trev taking his death particularly hard? Did something happen out there in the white that he doesn't want to talk about? Another part of him (the part that made his stomach turn and his chest heavy) asks another question: *what is his terrible secret?*

"Do you think we're safe here?" David asks.

Rhonda stands beside Doc, looking out the plate glass window as the white shifts and scatters. Zack is between them. Zack knows something. He is just a teenager, and every emotion shows blatantly on his face. He practically made an "Uh-oh, here we go" with his eyes when David asked about Alex. Zack knows the secret.

David stands to the side, looking out, trying to see beyond the curtain of white, but he cannot see more than a short distance in front of his nose. No one knows. Something very large might trudge right down the street in front of them and they might never know. Something might erupt from the white and grab them all before they have time to scramble away. Maybe there is no such thing as safe. Maybe you never really know.

"Roman said the thing in the white is looking for raw materials,"

Zack says. "It's building some sort of wall to keep us in. A pen, I guess. That is why the largest buildings were the first to go. The mayor seemed to think that City Hall was next in line. So we should be safe here."

"*Should*, huh? Not very reassuring."

Zack shrugs. "Unless the church was enough to finish the wall. Then I suppose it doesn't matter what building is next."

"You are not known for your rosy optimism, are you, Zack?" David quips.

Doc gives him a meaningful look. Touchy subject then.

"See anyone out there?" David asks instead.

"Not a single thing," Rhonda answers. "It seems everyone found a place to hide."

"Do you want to try and find other survivors?" Zack asks.

Doc looks back at the unconscious man on the table. "If Roman doesn't wake up, we need someone else who can tell us how to get the hell around a predator that has us trapped."

Zack looks out into the white. "There might be other locals holed up along here. There are businesses all up and down the street."

"That means going back out into the white," Doc says coldly.

"Not necessarily," Zack says, looking up and around. "The diner sets directly adjacent to the bank. The bank connects to the quick mart. Then to the pub on the corner. They are all joined by a corridor that runs along the alleyway so that in weather like this you can get from the diner to the pub without stumbling through the wind and snow."

"These businesses are all under one roof?" David inquires.

Zack looks at him. "Yes."

"Would you say that, all together, these interconnected businesses might be bigger than City Hall?" Doc extrapolates, following David's disheartening train of logic.

"City Hall is taller," Zack says.

"I'm not talking *taller*," Doc snaps. "Which one has more raw materials?"

"You can tell from the roof of the Resort. Or you could tell, I guess," Zack says. "I'd go up there sometimes when Mom was working. To think. This place takes up the whole block. So, I suppose it's this one."

Zack's eyes open wide as he realizes what he's saying.

"Aw, fuck," swears David.

And as one, the four of them step away from the front window. Rhonda rushes to Esther, gathering the old woman to her and pulling on the mittens and hats that will protect them against the cold. It will do no good to avoid the monster if it means freezing to death first. Doc rushes to Aspen, who is standing vigil over Roman at the table. Zack trudges behind her like a loyal puppy.

David finds Trevin, trying to locate some food in the kitchen. He has his hands full of energy bars. "Found these," he says.

"It's coming," David answers.

"Where's Zack?" Trevin says immediately, stuffing snacks into the pockets of his expensive ski jacket. He sounds almost panicked about it. Trev sprints toward the doorway to the main diner.

Zack and Rhonda have managed to get Roman vertical. "He's too heavy," Rhonda warns. "Trevin, maybe you can help m—"

"Leave him," Trevin interrupts. "He'll only slow us down. C'mon, Zack, we gotta run!"

"We aren't leaving him," Aspen screams.

Trevin looks at Zack. Zack looks at Aspen. And David waits for Trev to realize that the kid isn't leaving without the pretty young woman. It is the only reason Trev grits his teeth together and takes Zack's place under Roman's arm. Trev is the only other choice. With just one good arm, David is no help at all. So Trev and Rhonda stumble forward, almost toppling beneath their burden. How are they going to manage to get Roman through the snow if they cannot cross linoleum?

Doc steps up in front of Roman's lolling head and winds up, cracking her palm in a hard slap across his bearded face. Roman snaps awake, flailing, knocking Trev backward and toppling forward, taking Rhonda with him. They manage to both land on their hands and knees.

"Trouble?" Roman hisses.

"It's coming," Doc answers.

Roman nods. He manages to get to his feet on his own, tottering but not falling. Doc and Aspen help him reclose his bearskin coat. Doc cinches it tight with a leather strap. Roman grunts, then nods. Then all eight move toward the backdoor.

David goes first, opening the backdoor. The blast of cold is like a storm of knives cutting into the exposed flesh on David's face. He pulls the ski mask over his face until just his eyes are exposed, squinting against the wind and snow.

Fuckfuckfuck, David thinks. Swirling snow obscures everything in front of him. David doesn't want to see anyway. Trev grips his good hand tightly. Zack is on Trev's other side, and Trev has the kid by the arm.

"Wait," Roman warbles in a hoarse whisper, suddenly beside David.

The sound of ripping timbers and cracking foundations growl behind them. David slowly turns, looking back, through the slit in his ski mask like a frightened teenager would watch a slasher flick: horror-struck through the fingers of hands slapped over his face. Through a thousand shades of white, he glimpses an occasional survivor escape the interconnected buildings along the block, fleeing into the street, then being swept up by the thing in the snow. Like watching for an ace while someone shuffles a deck of cards, David spots someone in the whirling white here and there as they are plucked like weeds from the alabaster garden, defying gravity and logic.

Then the trickle of escapees abates. No one else runs out into the street. David sees something as big as a semitrailer sweep across the street, a blur of white within a blur of whiter. Something, then gone, then nothing.

A foot.

The old deputy drowning his destiny in whiskey said it was something from the future. Someone from the government said so, too, but the government told lies for a living. Zack said the internet gave the same story. The internet believes in UFOs and Sasquatch, too. The thing that was out there, in front of his eyes, was not from some terrible future, but right here and right now.

"Now," Roman says, as if agreeing with David's thoughts.

David is closest to the street, and he hesitates for just a moment. Long enough for Trevin to take the initiative, pushing Zack out in front of him. David is right behind them. He can't see anyone else out on the street. David understands Roman's plan: the first trickle of people escaping from the building were decoys. The monster anticipated those people. It plucked them as easily as bright blueberries on a perfectly white backdrop. Now the monster had moved on.

For now.

-29°

When Aspen was a kid, she had suffered terrible nightmares. After she'd wandered down to her mother's bedroom with tears streaming down her face and shaking like a leaf, Mother had explained that dreams were merely neurons firing in Aspen's mind and nightmares were just the vomit of the limbic part of the brain. "Your dorsal lateral prefrontal cortex is taking the backseat. So logic is just along for the ride. Go back to sleep, and the whole thing resets." As though Aspen had been a glitchy laptop rather than her flesh-and-blood daughter.

A recurring nightmare had involved dragons. Not the epic fantasy kind of dragons like in *Harry Potter* or *Lord of the Rings*. Neither Pete's nor Puff. The dragons in Aspen's nightmares had been the twisty snakes of Chinese lore. Like the slinky creatures one sees at a parade, weaving through the crowd in bright colors and as long as a semitrailer. Her mother had blamed the limbic, but there had been something else causing the dream, as it came back again and again over the course of many years. Now, in the middle of the white, on the top of a mountain in Montana, she finds herself face to face with a serpentine dragon.

Her breath hitches and she freezes, standing still as stone.

The dragon is white. Tangled like a ball of yarn, it is as still as Aspen, staring back. As the wind whines around her and flakes as fat as her fist fall from the sky, she doesn't move. The dragon is the color of the blizzard, blending in as she looks back, perhaps stretching on forever in the distance. All those years ago, the dreams had been warning her of this moment. The thing in the white is the thing from her nightmares. Now she stares it down.

"Aspen," her mother says, so close she snaps Aspen back to reality. This is no dream, then. Her mother is never in her dreams. She has never saved her from her nightmares.

"I thought it was the dragon," Aspen cries into the wailing storm.

"What?"

"The dragon from my dreams."

"It isn't real," her mother shouts over the wind. "It is a symptom. Hypothermia is setting in. We need to get you warmed up."

"That's what you said," Aspen moans, stumbling forward a step. "You always said it wasn't real."

"It's not, sweetheart. It's made of snow. A drift over a line of snow-bound cars."

"You were wrong," Aspen says, voice wavering and afraid. "You said monsters aren't real."

"Yes, I was wrong," her mother confesses, maybe saying those words for the first time in her whole life.

"Move, girl," comes a gruff, less-compassionate command. Roman takes Aspen by the elbow and practically shoves her past the snow dragon. He is the injured one, yet he is strong enough to keep her moving. So the dragon isn't real after all. Her mother is right about that. Just a trick of the white, a buried truck for a head, then a body made of cars, and a tail of a pair of blanketed snowmobiles.

Roman lurches forward as though each step might be his last. Rhonda is practically carrying Esther along the snowy road behind them. Trevin and David and Zack are ahead of them. Her mother is beside her, holding her steady. They are all tied together by the same length of rope in a Highwayman's Hitch. It had served them well enough getting back to the diner. Only Roman had declined. "I won't lose you," he promised. Aspen knows he meant that if he falls over and dies, he isn't taking anyone else with him.

Aspen is shivering so badly that she stops talking for fear of biting her tongue with her chattering teeth.

They come upon a small ice cream shop that was abandoned by responsible parties: someone locked the front door when they left. But apparently, Trevin isn't the type to let locks deter him from momentary respite. He kicks out, heel striking the deadbolt lock. In this cold, it snaps like peanut brittle. The place might not be bigger than a public restroom, but it is shelter from the storm. Eight survivors pile inside.

"Will we be safe here?" Zack asks Roman.

"The thing in the white won't come for us. Not yet," Roman reassures. "This place is too small to serve any purpose."

"Until the wall is finished," Aspen's mother observes. "Then the hunt begins. So far, that abominable creature has been shaking the trees and harvesting any fruits that scatter to the ground. But once the wall pens us all inside, it will pluck all the stray berries from the branches and start snacking on the stores tucked away in nooks and crannies such as this."

"Yes," Roman confirms.

"We're going to freeze before that happens," Rhonda states, white cloud puffing out and suspending in the air, obscuring her a little.

Roman checks the small propane heater that serves the whole shop. It isn't working. "Gas main must be ruptured," he says. "There will be a lot of townsfolk without heat."

"S-s-so cold," Zack complains.

"You aren't going to freeze to death anytime soon," Roman snaps. "Be grateful we have shelter from the storm."

The temperature continues to plummet. Colder and colder. How cold can it get? How long can they live against the terrible temperatures? It never gets this cold in Portland. Her mother has had her arms around Aspen since they escaped the wind, and the shivering has subsided somewhat. The walls of the ice cream shop might stave off the worst of the effects, but the body heat generated between eight people cannot suffice to save them for long. Besides, after the wall is done, the thing in the white will tear through these thin walls like it is made of paper.

"What now?" Aspen's mother asks Roman.

She knows how to doctor. She knows how to lead a team of surgeons. But she doesn't know how to survive this storm...or the thing in the storm. None of them know what will happen next.

Aspen looks to Roman. They all do. Smelly and sour, neither personable nor polite, he nevertheless knows how to survive. He saved Aspen. Maybe he can save them all. The monster is savage and cunning. Nothing civilized about it. More like Roman than the rest. The Mountain Man is the only one who can maybe understand it enough to avoid it.

"I have a plan," Roman reveals. "We stay here until it harvests more raw materials. We wait until the sonic boom blast signals it has moved on. Then we need to leave this shelter."

"The thunder," Rhonda wonders. "Why does it let us know it is safe to move around?"

"Maybe it is another kind of trap," Roman postulates. "Training us to react. Conditioning us to make us think we are safe when we hear the rumble, and then use it as a lure when the wall is done."

"It's just an animal," David argues. "From the future or not, it can't be planning ahead like that, can it?"

"It's not just an animal," Roman says darkly, putting his hand to his side where he was punctured.

"So what is this plan?" Aspen's mother asks, always looking to solve the problem, always trying to find a logical solution to a nightmare situation. But Aspen knows that sometimes you can't just wake up from a bad dream. Sometimes the dragons don't go away. The monsters are real.

"We need to find as many other survivors as we can," Roman says. "Whoever is left."

"Maybe most of them escaped already," Trevin suggests.

"No one has gotten out," Roman answers coldly. "Not yet, anyway."

"You don't know that," Trevin says. "Others could have gotten out when that thing was razing the resort, or the school or church, or even just now while it ripped up the diner."

"No," Roman says. "No one got out. Because there is another one. And it patrols the wall and monitors the gap in the fence."

Oh God, Aspen thinks. Her worst nightmares. One dragon hunts her in a recurring dream, slithering after her as she runs and runs and runs. Snaking through obstacles and winding around impediments, it chases her relentlessly. Another dragon waits at the end so that there is one in front of her and one behind her. Before she wakes, one always eats her. Either one or the other.

Go back to sleep, and the whole thing resets.

But this is not a dream. Aspen isn't asleep. She is awake. And the dragons are real. The danger is everywhere.

Roman puts words to her fears: "There are *two* things in the white."

-30°

Esther stares out a small, clear opening that is the only section not iced over by the hoarfrost covering the glass front of the ice cream shop. The irony of being saved from hypothermia by a place that serves cold is not lost on her. The thought of a three-scoop cone of pistachio both makes her stomach rumble and her flesh shiver all over again. The transparent space in the frost is the size of her numb hand. Beyond, white changes the shape of things: ghosts appear then disappear, elusive as her mercurial memories.

She is not alone. The black woman who insists on saving Esther from the storm remains behind at the ice cream shop. The rest are gone. Into the white. Following the plan. Esther does not recall the specifics, of either the plan or the past, but she remembers some things, like shapes outside revealed occasionally and suddenly by the blowing blizzard. *Walter, her husband. She lost Clarice Otter in the white. Stay away from City Hall.*

What's-her-name appears beside her with a bundle of clothes. There is a sweater that looks like it had been knitted by someone with a lot of time and limited skill. A handful of gloves. A fur hat that might have been left behind by a touristing Cossack. Purple earmuffs with cartoon characters on the fuzzy material, a superhero that looks like a robot whose name Esther probably never knew.

"I found these. There was a small lost-and-found box behind the counter," What's-her-name says. "I think we need to add a few layers before we go back out."

Esther shivers again. This time, it is not because of the cold. The thought of returning to the white is terrifying. She wonders if she goes back out into the snowstorm, will it might be the last thing she ever does. She will probably die before long out in the blizzard; she will certainly die after a while here in the shop.

What's-her-name pulls off the gloves Esther has used since they escaped the resort. She holds Esther's hands in her own, flesh against flesh, but it is just more cold against more cold. There is a limited amount of heat left in the world, and both of the women are depleted. Esther has avoided eye contact with other people ever since she started to lose her memory. She does not want What's-her-name to see the confusion in her eyes. And Esther does not want to see the concern in What's-her-name's gaze.

"Can you feel my hands?"

"They're cold," Esther answers.

"Are any of your fingers still numb?"

"No," Esther lies. The truth would not help. If she has frostbite, the future of her fingers is the same whether she tells What's-her-name or not. Her life still has the slimmest chance of being saved, but some of her fingers and toes are certainly going to be lost forever. Like Clarice. Like Walter. Like the memories wiped away by the cold, terrible white of her mind.

What's-her-name pulls thin cotton gloves over her fingers. Esther does not bother to count how many she can still feel. Then thick mismatched mittens are applied over the tops. Two layers on each hand.

"Do you believe it?" Esther asks.

What's-her-name does not look at Esther, as if she is afraid of the truth in Esther's eyes. "About what's out there?"

Esther nods as ear muffs are placed over her head. Will the superhero stave off the killer frostbite, or will she lose an ear as well as some fingers and toes? She can't count on a superhero to save the day. She just has this woman whose name she cannot recall.

"Do you really think it is some monster from the future?" Esther wonders.

"Did you notice how easy it was to convince the younger ones of what's out there?" What's-her-name asks. "Zack and Aspen accept it so easily. A creature from the future. Sure it is."

Esther helps pull on the Cossack hat. There were no other boots in the lost-and-found box, so her feet are still suffering in the boots she's been wearing since the beginning. Esther tries to wiggle toes that might as well have been the appendix she'd had removed when she was a teenager.

Her coat is adequate, and What's-her-name zips her up and checks her cuffs as if Esther is a toddler and the woman is a mother getting ready to send her eldest off into the dangerous world. A mask built into the collar pulls up and over her mouth. All that shows is Esther's eyes, and What's-her-name avoids looking at those.

"You could move faster without me," Esther says. Something about just sitting in the corner wrapped up in her attire seems alluring. She is so tired of moving forward, feeling her way through a fog of forgetfulness. It started long before the first flakes fell on Zukunft Falls. It has been going on for a few winters now. The white has been swallowing Esther up for a long time.

"Not a chance. We have a plan."

Esther sighs. "It's the future out there."

"It sure as hell isn't in here."

Esther looks around. She came to this place with Clarice Otter because she refused to fold to forgetfulness. Esther could still remember Walter. And Walter would not stop. He would not sit. He would keep moving on. Into the future.

And that's what gets her to move. Walter. Who else would remember Walter if she perishes in the storm? That's the damn problem. She doesn't know the answer. Clarice Otter knew Walter. But who else? Esther isn't even sure if they had kids who would remember him.

She might be the only person alive who can preserve the memory of her late lost love. So she will survive. To tell the tale of Walter to What's-her-name. So he is not forgotten forever.

"Okay," Esther concedes.

"Roman and the others will be at the rendezvous point soon. It is time to go," What's-her-name says. That is the plan, even if Esther can't remember the specifics. "Ready?"

"I know we can't stay," Esther sighs. "We have to go forward."

What's-her-name nods.

"And the plan?" Esther asks.

"The only way anyone is going to get out is if everyone doesn't get out."

Esther doesn't answer. She does not remember the details. *Stay away from City Hall.* That is what the big man who looks like a bear said before he left with the others. They had a mission. What's-her-name just has Esther. They had to go east.

Esther takes one last look out of the small clear spot on the glass facing the street. The hoarfrost has crept in even more; now it's just a peephole to the outside world as big as the thumb that would surely be amputated if she survives this snowstorm. White on white whipped up with white whirling white.

"Monsters from the future, huh?" Esther mumbles as What's-her-name pushes open the door and the wind blasts them in the chest, as solid as any wall. "It would be nice if I could forget about that."

-31°

Zack had wanted to pair up with the pretty Aspen Wang, but the young woman had picked Roman before Zack could even utter an invitation. He felt like he'd been picked last again for kickball, standing alone like the cheese in that fucking "Farmer in the Dell" song. Trevin and David were coupled, of course. Rhonda had to make sure she took care of Esther. He had thought Aspen would have automatically picked her mother, so Zack had hesitated, and Aspen had paired with Roman. That had left Zack with Dr. Wang.

"I was always picked last for basketball," Dr. Wang said, smiling. She was only five foot tall.

They make their way down Lewis and Clark Lane, working their way east, knocking on the door to every home or checking for inhabitants in every place of business. Some are empty. Some do not answer. Zack peers through the windows of many of the businesses along the way; he sees shadows move inside like things skulking in the white, but sometimes no one answers. Some have given up. Hiding. Hoping it will just go away.

Like the nasty posts online, things that are evil do not just go away. You have to do something about it.

Most of the folks who do answer their doors resist what Zack and Dr. Wang have to say at first, but Dr. Wang is persuasive. She has the authoritative tone of a doctor who has had to convince many a patient to endure painful treatments in order to cure a disease or recover from an injury. Zack prepares her with as many names as he can remember as they go from door to door, and Dr. Wang uses their names repeatedly, as if she has known them as long as Zack.

Some are unfazed by her arguments, insistent on hunkering down. Mr. Jolie from the bank scowls at the small woman like she is a child trying to tell the grown-ups what to do. His daughter, Eden, is Zack's age and appears in the entryway behind her father at the end of the argument, about the time Dr. Wang is telling Mr. Jolie that the prognosis for his family is imminent death. Eden puckers her fussy face and snorts at Zack. "Like we would listen to anyone wandering around in a blizzard with the Gurp."

Dr. Wang turns and stalks away. "Maybe some folks deserve to be eaten," she huffs.

Zack watches the white as they near the end of Lewis and Clark Lane. The mission is to warn as many people as possible to meet at the cafe. Roman had told them before they'd split up to rendezvous at Kaffe's Coffee Cafe in half an hour. They still have a couple of minutes left to stop at the final home along the street. Zack worries that it has been too long since the last baritone blast. Roman is sure that the next target is City Hall, all the way on the other side of town, but Zack still stares into the driven snow, looking for unearthly shapes or unexplained shadows. The wind whips the white like froth, thick as frosting on a birthday cake.

This morning, he had thought he might never see another birthday. This evening, he thinks he might never see another birthday. The gun pressed in the folds of flesh overflowing his waistband was set to be the end of him just hours ago, and now it might be the last resort if something comes out of the white and snatches him up. Same bullet, different circumstances. Zack does not want to die anymore. Now, if he eats a bullet, it will be with regret rather than relief.

"This is where Gertrude Hanks lives. She was my third-grade teacher."

Mrs. Hanks answers the door. Always sweet as a content old hen, she looks like she's aged fifty years in the time since Zack had learned phonics in her cheery classroom. She can't be more than sixty but seems a hundred. Her face is thin and birdlike, more like a vulture now than a cheerful chicken. Darkness falls across a face that had always been full of joy. Zack remembered her infinite zeal for learning. Sometimes you learn something you cannot unlearn.

"Go away," Mrs. Hanks snaps.

"Gertrude," Dr. Wang continues, as if she is the teacher and Gertrude Hanks is the unruly student. "The only chance to survive whatever the hell is happening in your town is to do something. You can't fight. You can't hide."

"They say it is a creature from the future," Mrs. Hanks clucks. "Zakaria, do you believe such nonsense?"

"It makes as much sense as anything else, ma'am," Zack replies with a shrug.

"I think the government is testing out some new weapon," the old teacher says. "They must be targeting some terrorist hiding in Zukunft Falls."

"Whatever it is, you cannot wait it out," Dr. Wang warns. "So you need to run."

"We are patriots in this house," Mrs. Hanks croaks, like an old crone instead of a kindly educator. "There is nothing to fear from the United States military!"

A little girl peeks from behind Mrs. Hanks's rumpled skirt. She is maybe four. She comes around to stand beside Mrs. Hanks, hugging herself against the cold wind coming in the front door. "Gramma?"

Mrs. Hanks tries to shut the door in Dr. Wang's face, but the doctor puts her foot between the panel and the jamb. Dr. Wang may be small, but she is stubborn. She shoves, the door flying wide, and Gertrude Hanks stumbles back.

"I am taking the kid with me," Dr. Wang says.

"Over my dead body," Gertrude Hanks sneers, spittle flying, looking more animalistic than grandmotherly.

Zack looks at that little girl. He thinks of his mother, who is probably dead. She'd always thought she'd been protecting him, giving him food whenever he was sad, letting him glower because he was "in a mood," making an appointment to see a psychiatrist and backing down when Zack had refused to go. In the end, trying to protect him had brought him to the brink of suicide. Now, he is still going to die. Probably sooner than later. And probably a hell of a lot more horribly than a bullet in the brain. He imagines this little girl getting taken by the thing in the white.

Dr. Wang takes a step forward, and Mrs. Hanks scratches at her like a cat protecting her kittens. The kindly third-grade teacher who had read *Green Eggs and Ham* and sang "The Whoopsie-Daisy Song" bares her teeth and actually hisses.

"Missus Hanks," Zack says calmly. "We are taking the kid with us. You are welcome to join us."

Zack does not really remember taking the gun out of the waistband of his pants, but it is in his hand and pointing at Mrs. Hanks. He is shaking, but at this range, there is no way Zack could miss if he pulls the trigger. The fight goes out of the old woman. She collapses, sobbing, to the floor. Dr. Wang takes a small winter coat from the entryway closet and helps the little girl into it. She fits the girl with other stuff from the closet: mittens and muffs, snow pants and a scarf, hat, and boots.

"Come on, Missus Hanks," Zack cajoles, still aiming the gun at her. "Get a coat on. And a hat."

She doesn't answer. She just sobs. Mrs. Hanks has given up. Zack knows the feeling.

The little girl is bundled up, and when Dr. Wang offers her a hand, she takes it. Just four, and she already knows who is fighting and who is giving up. The kid wants to fight.

"We are meeting at Kaffe's if you screw up some courage, Missus Hanks. You taught me the difference between 'farther' and 'further' when I was nine. Well, it is just a little farther. I will wait for you as long as I can. But I can't wait too long. Because I don't want to die anymore, Missus Hanks."

He turns and follows Dr. Wang as she leads the little girl into the white. Aspen's mother stops and looks at him. She heard what he said. Zack thinks she had already had an inkling, but now she has heard it out loud. Not half a day ago, Zack had planned on ending his own life. Only seventeen and done with this world. Her eyes convey a breaking heart.

If the only casualty she suffers this day is that, then it will be a miracle.

But, of course, this is a world where monsters skulk in the white and cold gets so severe it threatens to turn blood to ice and there is a wall of refuse surrounding the entire city.

This is a world without miracles.

-32°

Roman's plan.

They are not all going to make it. Roman and Aspen had gone up and down residential streets, telling everyone who would answer their door to meet on the east side of town. "The next time the thunder sounds, we run. East. There's a wall. We climb, up and over."

They hadn't told anyone about the other monster in the white.

How many will show? *Enough*, Roman believes. The only way that anyone will survive is if they all go at the same time. If there are too many targets to manage. Like ants all erupting at once from a hill, scurrying across the sand, more than even two giants can stomp before some of them get far enough away.

At least, that is the plan.

"And why do we need to sacrifice everyone in City Hall?" Aspen shouts over the storm as they cross from one street to the adjacent one, past the place where the school had once stood. The world beyond two feet in front of them is just white. He keeps Aspen close as they move house to house.

"Because it will know we are planning something," Roman answers. "If the thing in the white disassembles City Hall and there are no people inside, it will know we have a plan."

"It will *know?*" Aspen challenges. "Do you believe what they are saying? That it is something from the future? A monster that broke through time?"

"I don't believe anything," Roman grumbles against the wind. "I know what I know. The rest doesn't matter."

"It doesn't matter where it comes from? Or when? Won't the facts help us formulate a successful plan?"

"Survival doesn't depend on what anyone is going to tell me," Roman says. "The only thing that matters is what I know. What I see. What I can touch and watch and *hunt.* You can read all the stories you want about how to fight a bear, but it isn't going to prepare you for fighting a *fucking bear.*"

Aspen stares at the furs covering Roman. "You fought a bear?"

"It was him or me," Roman mumbles. "That's always the nature of nature."

"Hence, the plan," Aspen says. "Them or us. Human sacrifice."

"Diversion."

Instead of wrinkling her nose, Aspen nods. She understands.

City Hall was on the west edge of Zukunft Falls. And Roman is sure by now that the proper tense is "was." It has been quiet for nearly an hour since the last attack. If Roman's calculations are correct, the materials from the diner and its adjoining structures were enough to fill the gap that the mayor and the woman in the eyepatch tried to escape through. If the thing in the white is efficient, and Roman believes it is damn efficient, then it will use the materials from City Hall to reinforce the west wall. Once the entire perimeter is secure, then the monsters will purge the rest of the town of prey. Like shooting fish in a barrel.

Roman had left civilization to get away from computers and robots and satellites and automation. Since he has been gone, phones have become an addiction and celebrities are treated as amoral royalty and politics is comic relief. No one speaks to one another anymore; they just post faceless insults on social media. He does not know how any of it works; Roman just knows that none of it works. He'd been right to get away.

This cold may be from some experiment gone awry or an alien ship from the frigid far reaches of space. Wherever it came from, it doesn't matter. He knows enough about predators. Hunters and prey. He knows how to survive.

Now Roman and Aspen move through the blizzard, along the street, house to house in systematic warning. Roman needs to get as many people to escape at the same time as possible. Every additional body increases the odds for success.

Him or me. Them or us. The nature of nature.

Then it comes out of the white, fast and from nowhere, appearing like magic. Roman is cold and hurt, his reflexes no longer quick enough to react before it could disappear again into the white. But Aspen is young and swift, and she steps in front of the figure racing eastward. Taller than her by a head and a half, the sprinting boy plows into her, and they both hit the snowy street in a tangle of limbs.

Roman reaches down and pulls the kid up by the scruff of his neck. He holds his puncture wound with his other hand, pain seizing the whole side of his body. Roman winces but does not flinch. Skinny and tall, this kid is mostly legs and arms. Built for running. Already whiter than white, the winter and stark fear have made him paler, like a ghost fleeing through a cloud.

Aspen stands up, brushing snow too cold to melt off of her outerwear. She looks up at the boy who is about her age. "What're you running from?" she asks over the whine of wind. Like she doesn't know.

"That thing," the kid says, staring over his shoulder into the white.

"You came from City Hall?" Roman asks.

The tall kid nods.

"How many people are holed up there?" Aspen wonders.

"Too many." The kid shudders. The temperature has dropped within the last few seconds.

Roman would not have asked. It is usually better not to know. The sacrifice was necessary. Roman and Aspen had already warned several households. Between David and his fiancé, and the fat kid with the doctor, each pair would have warned just as many as Roman and Aspen. The ones that were interested were instructed to tell others. Roman's plan may give the most possible people a chance to survive.

They work down the last street on their list. The tall kid follows Aspen like a lost puppy looking for a new master. They are of a same age, and romance has been born under less oddball circumstances, but Aspen regards the young man with no more interest than the parade of people they present with Roman's plan. It is Roman she responds to, a spark in her eye like a female has not favored him with in many, many years. He had saved her life. And she loves him a little for it. A little is more than he has deserved for decades.

Time's up. They make their way to the rendezvous point. Kaffe's Coffee Cafe contains everyone Roman knows in the whole world, in addition to a half dozen strangers who have straggled in to find shelter from the cold. It is here that they will wait for the sound to send them rushing toward the end, that gunshot that starts the final sprint, the crack of thunder that breaks through the fear and anticipation and sends the ones with a fighting spirit forward, onward, for at least a chance to live.

Aspen reunites with her mother. The obese teenager sits at a small table with the doctor. The tall kid from City Hall gives the fat kid a scowl and joins some locals behind the counter between modern coffee machines and a glass case filled with pastries. Trevin and his mate sit across from each other in a small booth. The old woman wrings her hands and paces in a small circle in an open spot in front of a community bulletin board that advertises skiing lessons given by an instructor who might be dead and an announcement for a seniors' dance next weekend at the school gym, certainly canceled in light of current events. Rhonda stands near the exit as Roman surveys the crowd. She stares out the front window, looking for something in the white. Escape? Answers? Something she might never find.

"Do you think anyone else is going to try to escape?" Rhonda asks.

"I am sure of it," Roman answers. "I left the world because it was turning into something I didn't recognize. Gadgets and gizmos ruled the day. Animosity was everywhere. Then something inside me kicked in. An instinct to rebel against extinction. To survive. Maybe I saw the signs of Armageddon twenty years ago when most people didn't. But there is no missing the signs this time. People want to survive. And this kind of devastation is right in their faces. I see the fire in their eyes. Do you see it?"

Rhonda nods. "We shall find out soon enough."

They stand side by side, searching the white for signs. But the snow shifts, revealing nothing, the next moment as obscure as the far future. The next second as unpredictable as a hundred years from now. The blast of baritone thunder will be the shot of the starting pistol that will herald the rest of their lives. Be their future long or short.

-33°

Rhonda stares out the plate glass window that faces east. Any minute now, momentum would overtake the moment and she will be moving, running, racing to the end. The thermometer hanging on the outside of the window is a mercury type, existing in defiance to a digital world, registering lows the likes that Rhonda Phelps has never seen. Thirty-two is the freezing point, but that is on the other side of zero. A long, long way away from a thaw.

Has she ever been so cold?

She hugs herself and shivers. Rhonda glances at Esther, huddled between Aspen and David for warmth. The signs of hypothermia have faded, but Rhonda still believes Esther is lying about the feeling in her extremities. A hospital has to be in their near future. If there is a future out there beyond frozen monsters.

Xueman steps up beside Rhonda. "I need your help," the doctor says.

The women are of an age. Rhonda has rarely talked to anyone from her own generation. She had always sought out a younger crowd, trying to integrate into a trendier group. It had made her feel livelier and hipper to tether herself to a generation one or two (or three; lately, it had been three) behind her own. Yesterday, Rhonda would have been more likely to party with Aspen than to talk to Aspen's mother. But now, when she looks into Xueman's eyes, Rhonda sees something that she has been missing for a long time. Sisterhood. Understanding. The wisdom of experience shared between two women who have bonded under similar circumstances. It is nice.

"We aren't going to perform another surgery, are we?" Rhonda asks.

"No. Not medical kind of help. I need motherly kind of help."

"I've never been the motherly type," Rhonda confesses.

"I've seen you with Esther," Xueman dismisses. "You have the mothering instinct. The sense of protecting your herd."

"You need me to look out for Aspen?"

"No, she's got someone watching over her. I am talking about the little girl."

Xueman and Zack had brought a toddler back with them after they had all split into pairs. The little girl sits across from Esther, sipping hot cocoa, snuggled under Zack's thick arm for warmth, barely visible in the gloom of the interior lighted with just flickering candles. One determined barista warms coffee and tea and cocoa on a single burner that runs off of flame from a gas line that has avoided being ruptured by the systematic disassembly of the town.

"Her name is Samantha. If her parents are still alive, they could be anywhere. So we need to get her over the wall. She is too small to climb on her own, and I—"

"I'll get her over," Rhonda interrupts. She has seen Dr. Wang in action saving Roman's life. She has probably saved thousands in her career. She is fearless and fierce. But she is five feet tall and weighs all of a hundred pounds. There is no way she could take the pudgy four-year-old over the wall. David is injured. Roman is injured. Zack is going to have a hard getting himself let alone handling a passenger. Aspen isn't any bigger than her mother.

"Thanks," Xueman says. "I would ask Trevin, but..."

"I don't trust him either," Rhonda agrees. "Something happened out there in the white. I see the way Zack looks at him."

Xueman nods. Maybe it is women's intuition. Maybe it is just that wisdom of older women who have seen their fair share of douchebags in this world. They could not trust Trevin with Samantha's life.

"I need you to help Esther over, then," Rhonda says. "She will probably forget where she is going. And forget who you are. But she's my responsibility. She's my Samantha."

Xueman offers her hand to seal the deal. "We're not *guys*, Xueman," Rhonda scolds softly. "C'mere." She pulls the petite doctor into a smothering embrace. And the doc hugs her back.

Rhonda walks over to where Esther is asking little Samantha if she has any pets.

"Just stuffed ones," Samantha says. "I have a snowman named Carl, but I don't like him anymore. The snow is scary."

Rhonda puts a gentle hand on the girl's shoulder. "You know what my momma would tell me when I was little and scared of the dark?"

The little girl looks up at Rhonda and shakes her head.

"She would scoop me up and hold me tight. She whispered in my ear, 'Close your eyes tightly, my darling, and I will carry you through the night. And on the other side of the darkness, there is only light. When you open your eyes next, the world will be bright.' She would hold me and rock me back and forth until I fell fast asleep. When I opened my eyes again, every time, it was morning, and the sun was out, and the world was bright."

"That sounds nice," Samantha says.

It is nearly time. Rhonda starts to help both Samantha and Esther into their winter attire, applying every precaution against the bitter cold.

"How about you come with me when it is time to go?" Rhonda asks as she secures the zipper of the girl's collar, snug over her mouth. "I bet you can hold on like a strong girl."

Samantha nods. She flexes arms almost too stiff to bend in her multiple layers like a bodybuilder and issues a muffled, "*Real* strong."

Rhonda looks at Esther. Her face is exposed, so Rhonda wraps the gray scarf she got for her birthday around Esther's face. The old woman stares at Rhonda through the slit between her Cossack hat and woolen scarf like she is trying to remember her name.

"Xueman is going to help you over the wall while I take the little girl, Esther," Rhonda says.

"The doctor?"

"That's right," Rhonda assures.

"She seems nice."

"She is. She will make sure you get over safely. And then I will see you on the other side."

"I'm sorry, dear," Esther confesses, adjusting her thick mittens. "I don't remember your name."

The baritone bass sounds, the signal to make a run for it. Rhonda looks out into the white. "Names don't really matter right now." Rhonda opens her arms, and Samantha hops up. "How about I introduce myself after we make it to the other side?"

"I'll remember that," Esther says as Xueman rushes over and takes the old woman by the hand.

Roman and Aspen wait at the door. Zack stands with David, Trevin between them, gripping both of their hands. Samantha snuggles against Rhonda's shoulder. Rhonda zips the collar of her coat up over her chin, covering up the last bit of vulnerable skin. She is as ready as she can be.

Roman stands, staring at the white. "It's time," he declares.

Through the snow, shadows begin to appear. People running for the wall. More and more and more. Roman opens the door, and the inhabitants of Kaffe's Coffee Cafe start pouring out.

"Close your eyes tightly, my darling, and I will carry you through the night," Rhonda whispers in the little girl's ear. "And on the other side of the darkness, there is only light. When you open your eyes next, the world will be bright."

Then Rhonda is next.

The cold blasts through every layer.

Then Rhonda is in the white and wind, running, and she thinks that she might not see fifty after all. Tomorrow is her birthday, but tomorrow is whipped away, wiped clean by the white.

-34°

The cold cuts. The wind sighs like a sword slicing air. White blinds, so the world in front of them may be either endless or abruptly ending. Shadows scurry all around them, dark shapes manifesting from nothing and then dissolving like figments of imagination. Like a lost soul looking for the great beyond, white makes clouds all around as fellow spirits form and fade near or far, either everywhere or nowhere.

Trevin keeps the great bear in front of him. The burly black man should have been dead from being stabbed like that, but instead, he just goes on and on. Trev grasps David with his right hand, never letting go ever again. Zack's chubby paw is in his left hand, Trevin dragging him behind like a shiny lure at the end of a fishing line just in case a monster in the white decides to try a bite.

How many? The silhouettes dancing outside the alabaster veil number dozens. Are some the same or are they all individual? Extrapolating across the entire eastern side of the city, if the shadows indicate the number currently racing toward the wall, then the population choosing to take their chances at escape might number a hundred. Even with his chunky insurance policy in his left hand, if there were only a dozen people that tried to make it over the wall, then he would likely be dead by dawn. But if Trevin is one out of a hundred? He liked those odds.

Maybe he will live.

Probably, he will live.

And David would probably live with him.

The bear stops suddenly. A deeper shadow appears as David slows, a more substantial shape static in the stuttering white. The wall. It looms before them, reaching up into the blizzard, stretching into the white. *A stairway to Heaven*, Trevin thinks, as an old rock song that his Grandad loved slinks through his head.

The first rung of the ladder to scale the wall is made up of a smashed sedan that looks like it was flattened by a crusher in a junkyard. David struggles to swing himself up one-armed. He still has that crazy-ass ice pick duct-taped to his forearm, but he refuses to remove it. Trevin boosts him from below, keeping one eye on Zack to make sure the hefty kid isn't scurrying up the wall in an adrenalized rush. Zack looks like a fat toddler trying to pull himself up onto a sofa.

Trevin hauls himself up on the hood of a Honda Civic, smoothed to no more than a foot thick, then reaches over to the trunk, where Zack has managed to only make it two inches off the ground. Trevin imagines a worm wriggling on a hook as he grabs Zack by the collar of his thick coat and pulls him up.

"Thanks," Zack huffs, and looks at Trevin like he is his savior.

Stupid kid. The bait thanking the fisherman. Trevin is using him, and Zack looks like he might want to be BFFs.

"Just keep close," Trevin snaps.

There are other climbers around them scaling the heap of piled debris. The wall acts as a windbreak, the people around him more substantial as the white thins in a slower swirl against the barrier. Some scurry up the side with haste, while others are deliberate. Then one disappears, a man to Trevin's right wearing a tan trench coat, like a detective looking for clues, plucked up and into the opaque sky. He screams briefly, as if telling the world that he has solved the case, then silence. The next level above the flattened Honda Civic is a section of the church, a painting of Jesus still attached to a slat-board wall. The Lord's eyes seemed to follow Trevin as he crosses a horizontal section, careful not to step on Jesus's face, to help Zack up to the next level. The painting seems to accuse Trevin of something he hasn't done yet.

A woman who looks about his mother's age pulls herself up onto the section of church wall, alone, scampering higher in a panicked scramble. She wears pink boots with lights that blink with every step, certainly something stolen off of someone else. Someone *younger*. Her jacket is inadequate for the elements, a thick housecoat more suited to sitting by the fire than fending off the fierce blizzard. No hat, no gloves. Her fingers are blue, her nose gray with frostbite. If she survives the wall, she will certainly lose part of it. Without pause or offer of help to a man with two lame companions slowing him down, she continues up the wall. Trevin watches the blinking pink lights ascend steadily as he boosts David up to the next level. She gets higher, higher, then suddenly she rises faster and even higher than the top of the wall. The lights blink, blink, blink, then disappear. Either obscured by the white or ingested by the thing inside the white.

"Move, move, move," Trevin calls, mostly hustling Zack. David is no faster than the fat kid with his one arm, but David is not Trev's protection against being the next one plucked off this wall.

Zack disappears over the lip of the next part of the barricade, a tangle of wood shakes from a section of roof roughly the size of a river raft. Then the world quakes, the wall shakes, as something bigger than anything that has ever moved upon this Earth slams the ground along the barricade like a child throwing a tantrum by stomping its feet. Trevin grasps a section of oak handrail sticking out horizontally from the debris, grabbing David with his other hand so his fiancé does not slip off the section and over the edge.

Trevin's eyes sweep the white. Smaller shadows move to each side, people briefly paused resuming their ascent. He looks outward from the wall, trying to see what cannot be seen: the next moment, the next threat, whatever might be there that can take David away. Last night, he was afraid of any kind of future with David. Now he is afraid of losing any kind of future at all.

"I...," David huffs, looking at the pathway upward that Zack just managed, "I don't think I can, Trev."

The impact shifted the debris that formed the wall. The footholds Zack had used to climb a level higher have collapsed and fallen away. Trevin would have to deadlift David some six feet vertically to reach the next ledge.

"You can," Trevin says. "You have to."

On his left, a shadow in the distance, then the shadow is gone, pulled outward into the white, the only epitaph a stunted scream.

"David…"

"What happened to Alex?" David asks.

Trevin exhales, the cold making crystals of his breath. The white fog hangs there between them. Like a cloud. Like something toxic frozen in time. It is so cold. So goddamn cold.

"This isn't the time for that."

"It *is* the time for that," David disagrees.

The wind stops for a second, and the driven snow is suddenly suspended, as if without the current of air it has no idea where to go. Fat flakes flutter in front of Trevin, twirling in place, not falling or fleeting or fluttering about. Just still. Frozen. The whole world frozen.

"I'm sorry, David. It was a mistake. It didn't mean anything. I was scared. Scared and stupid."

Trevin expects tears, but none come. He also expected to lie about it forever. Alex was not going to tell anymore. But confession came at the edge of Armageddon. David looks at him with those white flakes floating between them, ice in the air.

"I hope you will be able to forgive me, David," Trevin says, warm words across the cold space between them. "Just never forget that I love you with all my heart."

David looks away, into the white, maybe searching his heart. Maybe watching for an abrupt end. Then he turns back to Trevin.

"I will never forg—"

Forget? Forgive? The word is lost in the white. David disappears, snatched away before he gives the answer, gone in a swirl of snow. So fast, Trevin did not even have time to reach out. Trevin blinks. It is over. Just like that.

And then, too late, the tears come.

-35°

Aspen helps Roman up the side of the wall. He hardly needs it. Her mother seems to think the man ought to be incapacitated, or dead, but he plows forward like a relentless, stubborn machine. Like this blizzard itself, he is unyielding, unfazed. Aspen remains close to him to lend a hand if needed, but Aspen needs him more than he needs her. He saved her life. He is some kind of a superhero for saving her from the white.

They are leading the group up the wall. Roman first, Aspen right behind. Her mother is behind, somewhere. Aspen does not even think to worry about her. Her mother may be as tenacious as Roman, but she is the known quantity, and Roman is something new. Her mother is a protective tigress, but Roman is a roaring lion.

He looks like a bear. His coat is matted with ice and snow and blood and something sweet and sticky that seems alien. His face features fearsome determination, as if he is a god staring down the fates. Rugged and ruthless, he climbs and climbs, forward momentum personified, an irresistible force that has yet to meet an immovable object.

Rhonda and the little girl her mother kidnapped are directly behind Aspen. She sees them when she looks back, flickering in the white like something in shadow intermittently revealed by sunlight. Rhonda pauses occasionally to lift Samantha to the next level or to carry her across a precarious section of the debris. Roman had picked this part of the wall because it started zigzagging back and forth from the ground up like a handicap ramp slowly ascending in elevation.

Then they are in a bathroom.

Tile floor. Pastel walls. Bisque toilet missing its tank. Bathtub full of snow. A mirror still hangs on the wall over the basin, reflecting white and white and more white. Fifteen feet in the air, one section is completely gone and opens over the edge of the wall. In the opposite direction, a door leads to a Ford folded in half. Through a window missing its glass, Aspen stares out at a section of parking lot turned vertical. Out the wide open way, the end is there, either inches away or waiting for later. It always is.

"We wait here for the others," Roman says.

"We are almost at the top?"

Roman nods.

Aspen nods her understanding.

They need to all go over together. The top of the wall is the most dangerous part. Easy pickings.

Aspen and Roman each grab a hand and help Rhonda up. She slides Samantha around in front of her and hugs the little girl, sharing her warmth. She does not ask why they have paused. She knows. Rhonda looks back over the edge, searching for Esther. Aspen's mother promised Rhonda that she would watch over the old woman.

People pass them on either side, shadowy forms ascending level by level. Up and up and over. Some of them disappear before they get to the top, either erased by a bluster of snow or taken by something else in the white. Some scream when they are plucked away. Others go silently.

Then shadows appear below, two figures climbing slowly up the side. *Mom?* Aspen wonders. One shape grows and grows, resolving itself into obesity. Zack groans as he gets close, sounding like a man suffering multiple injuries instead of mere physical exertion. Trevin is right beside him, moving slowly to keep pace with the struggling climber.

No one asks about David. There is only one answer.

Aspen and Rhonda stare into the white. Zack sits in the corner, still huffing and puffing. Roman stands sentry, arms folded in front of him, waiting.

"We need to keep moving," Trevin says. "We're sitting ducks here."

"Not without my mother," Aspen declares.

"Then we will all be dead," Trevin grumbles.

"He's right," Roman agrees. "Time to move on."

Aspen looks at Roman like she might have heard him wrong. He is the hero. He saved her. He can't mean to leave her mother and Esther behind.

"I'll go back," Roman says. "See if they need help."

He did not add an "or," but Aspen fills it in.

"You could barely manage the climb up on your own," she points out.

"I will manage just fine."

Trevin is already lifting himself over the top edge of the wall. He pulls Zack up behind him. Rhonda boosts Samantha up after Zack and starts pulling herself up.

"I'm going with you," Aspen decides.

Roman pauses. He looks at her. Really looks at her. And Aspen realizes he is no superhero. No god. Not some feral bear protecting an adopted cub. He is just a man. Fear tinges his brown eyes.

"I never had a kid, but I know any mother would never want her daughter rushing into danger to save her life. Her job is to make sure you are okay, not the other way around. You cannot risk it, Aspen. Your mom wants you to live. That's why she sent you with me. I didn't need help getting up this wall, kiddo. She just said that so you'd go. She expects me to make sure you get to the other side."

"I'm not leaving her," Aspen says, tears threatening to spill out and freeze her eyelids shut.

"You're not. I will get her. I'll make sure she gets over. Just like I am going to make sure you get over."

Aspen doesn't understand in time to dodge his quick grab. His hand is like a steel manacle locked on her forearm. She faces him, like prey caught by a predator, trapped, nowhere to run. No less freedom than if she'd been snatched by the thing in the white, Aspen is at his mercy.

"Save her," Aspen commands.

"I promise," Roman replies.

Aspen finally nods. Roman is right. He boosts her up around the outside lip of the detached bathroom, shoving her onto the next level, landing in a puff of snow between Rhonda and Zack.

Aspen stands, dusting off the back of her thick snow pants, then peers through a hole in the ceiling where a light fixture had once existed. Below, Roman walks to the edge of the tiled floor and looks down. He made a promise. Aspen believes it. He will find her mother and bring her back.

"Let's get down the other side of this wall before we get plucked off the top," Rhonda says, looking up into the shifting void above them. The wind howls, finding ways into even the layers and layers Aspen has applied to fend off the cold. Trevin has already disappeared over the lip of the wall, and Zack is starting down after him.

"I'm right behind you," Aspen promises.

She just wants to see Roman off. The man in fur winces as he grabs ahold of a bent handicap bar. He eases himself over the edge. In her head, Aspen wishes him Godspeed.

Then Roman disappears into the white.

Upward instead of down.

Aspen catches a brief glimpse of him as he zips past her into the obscure sky. *I'm sorry*, the look on his face seems to say. Then he is gone. Lost to the white. His promise to save her mother is just so much snow blowing in the wind.

The howl of the storm is matched only by the roar of Aspen's scream.

-36°

Last night, Zack had imagined all the ways he could kill himself. It was not the first time he had considered an end. His life had been one long stretch of darkness. That light at the end of the tunnel that is supposed to signify a brighter tomorrow had never manifested for Zack. All his tomorrows had been as black and bleak as all his todays. So he already had some methods that he had previously pondered: pills, hanging, using a tube and car exhaust, slitting his wrists and drifting off in the bathtub. The pistol in the basement had finally won out, dramatic and definite, and he had thought the idea of a paused suicide note posting to social media once his phone had returned to service would be darkly poetic, like his last message would live on after the end.

A close second had been throwing himself off Pike's Cliff up Bailey's Peak. That would be a death talked about for decades. Maybe the town would feel sorry enough to rename the drop-off Zakaria's Cliff in remembrance of the boy they had let down. Down, down, down. Zack had imagined falling and falling. He wondered what would happen if he had changed his mind halfway down. It is the same reason he had decided against pills or rope or razors. What if he had decided he didn't want to die after it had started? He shuddered at the thought of the ground rushing up after he decided he wanted to live. The gun afforded no second thoughts. The gun would splash his thoughts all over the basement wall.

Now Zack is near the top of the wall, looking down into the white, descending step by step. Oh so carefully. So many times, he had considered jumping to his death off Pike's Cliff. Now he is scared to death that he might slip and fall into the white. The only thing that keeps him moving is being more terrified of what is up than what is down. And Trevin.

"C'mon, Zack, stay close. You are the only thing I have left," Trevin calls, a few rungs down a ladder made of snapped two-by-fours and bent steel beams. "Jesus Christ, you are slower than that old lady the doctor got stuck with."

Rhonda has already disappeared, descending far enough below him to be obscured by the white. Aspen is behind him with Roman. Roman won't let anything happen to her, and Aspen knows it. Zack sees the way the girl looks at Roman. Like he is a fucking rock star or something. Jealousy sits heavy in his heart.

Zack can't reach the next platform. He dangles from a wooden beam that might have been what helped hold up the church roof once upon a time. His mittens are thick and clumsy, threatening to let his sweaty hands slide right out and leave his clammy paws to the elements, freezing the sweat instantly and giving him gloves of pure ice. If he loses his protection against the cold and wind and still manages to survive, he cannot imagine the teasing the Gurp will endure if, in addition to his other obvious deviations from normality, he also possessed stumps instead of hands. Zack drops down the last six inches, slips, and lands flat on his giant bottom, a statue of Mary, mother of Jesus, staring at him from the wall of debris.

Two virgins, frosting in the cold.

"God damn it, Zack, move that ass!"

Trevin is to the side, across a bridge made of sheetrock and timber. Zack gets up and staggers across the rickety span. Trevin hunkers down against the wind, waiting, unwilling to leave Zack too far behind. Zack tries. He tries because Trevin expects him to try. He cannot give up when someone else has such faith that he can make it. David and Alex are both gone. Like Trevin said, Zack is the only one he has left.

Thing, whispers that dark part of him that wrote the last words he planned to ever write before he picked up the gun to make his bloody signature. *Trevin said Zack is the only* thing *he has left.*

"Why are you working so hard to save me?" Zack asks over the whistling wind. Maybe for an answer. Maybe to buy a few seconds to catch his breath through the thick ski mask that covers his wide face.

"Everyone else is dead, kid," Trevin says. "I can't do this alone."

"I'm a stranger."

"Not anymore. You're more like a brother."

Just a *thing*, the dark part of him sneers.

Then it looms out of the white, so fast Zack surprises even himself by his fast reflexes. The shadow sweeps toward Trevin, and instead of cowering or running away or fainting in the face of fear, Zack steps toward it. He suddenly has his mitten off and the gun in his hand. He pulled it from his waistband and pointed at the white in the white, the thing in the nothing.

It is just a thing.

How had he drawn the weapon so fast? He had never moved so quickly in all his life.

Zack fires. Once, twice. Again. Again. The thing that intended to snatch Trevin steers instead toward Zack. Zack stumbles in retreat, firing again. It reaches, a hand as big as a coffin with white fur, like a polar bear, colder than the cold. What did the geeks at the comic book shop say it was? A creature born of achieving negative on the Kelvin scale. The other side of absolute zero. Zack's white death.

The paw keeps coming, grabbing. Zack dodges it and falls backward. Down. Down. Down. He lands in a snowbank at the base of the wall, deep enough to save him from broken bones. The paw descends after him, reaching, and Zack retreats against the base of the wall. He squeezes into a hovel braced by wire mesh and crisscrossed crucifixes, all wedged between a section of ceiling and pieces of splintered pews. The thing in the white grinds against the wall, making debris shift and the opening close with collapsing rubble. It digs for a minute, like an alien yeti the size of Godzilla, worrying the clogged opening, but eventually, it stops short of burrowing into the barrier. It will not risk destroying the barricade to snap up some tasty snack. Zack is deep enough inside the wall that he is safe. For now.

Safe from the monster.

The cold is still everywhere.

He is surrounded by debris. The only way out is back the way he entered, past the thing in the white.

"Zack?"

It's Trevin. His voice comes from outside the cave of carnage that suddenly feels more like a cell than salvation. Trevin has scaled down the wall and stands right outside. Zack cannot see him, but he is sure there is a ton of wreckage between him and Trevin. This is the second time today where Zack has been trapped somewhere that he could not easily escape.

"I'm alright," Zack calls out. "But I'm stuck."

Silence. Silence but for the backdrop of incessant wind and the intermittent screams somewhere in the distance. Because there are two of those monsters in the white.

Then, "Thanks for the save, kid. I'm sorry it has to end like this."

"Trevin, wait," Zack calls out, but the man who had said he was just a thing is already gone.

Zack is alone. The end comes like his end was always going to come. Just him. All alone. No one is coming to save him.

He looks at the pistol in his hand. His fingers are already numb. Blue. Freezing solid. It contains just one more bullet. A last chance to end it by choice rather than by ingestion. When the town is razed, the thing in the white will come back for him. When the wall is no longer necessary, the monsters will not hesitate to ruin their barrier for a tasty dessert like plump Zakaria Alaoui. If the cold does not get him first.

He hopes the cold gets him first.

If not, the bullet will serve. He will not have his last thought on Earth be the realization of what all those pieces of pie felt like when

Zack attacked half of one after dinner every other night. The last thing Zack is ever going to eat is a bullet.

He settles back. He takes the mitten from his warm hand and covers the frozen one. Zack takes his phone out of his pocket. Turns it on. He sets it on a shelf made of floor tile and shoves his bare hand as deeply into his coat pocket as possible. The smashed screen offers neither one last picture of his mom nor a comforting message from someone who had received his suicide note and wants him to know someone out there cares. Because no one cares. But at least the cracked glass affords a little incandescent light. Something to fend off the darkness. For a little while, at least.

-37°

Sometimes retreat is the only route to survival. Xueman has treated many patients over the years where she has had to back off and regroup. Her first assessment may have been incorrect, or the circumstances had changed as they moved forward so she has had to adjust, revise, redo. Sometimes she would have had to radically alter her approach, coming through the anterior instead of the posterior, or cutting instead of stitching, even amputating instead of repairing. So Xueman is never afraid to stop and go back.

She was five feet off the ground with Esther when she knew this section of wall was impossible. She would never have made it to the top with both of them still alive. So she had scaled back down, taking longer to reverse than they had going forward, and started to survey the perimeter of the wall. Xueman could only think of Aspen, climbing the barrier, probably already to the top. A thousand things could go wrong. One very large thing in the white could go wrong.

"Leave me," Esther had said again and again. "Your daughter needs you more than this old bag of bones."

She did not know if Esther was just stubborn, or if she forgot she said it each time right after it came out of her mouth.

"That's not how I work," Xueman had replied to every protestation.

Like her instincts that guided her true most of the time during surgery or diagnosis, she'd known the right place to try a second attempt at the wall. Xueman had recognized a booth from the diner where the thing in the white had almost got them. They had started to climb. The debris had happened to be randomly arranged in the shape of make-shift steps. Following juts and jags that acted as a wonky sort of stair-way, Xueman found the easiest path upward.

On each side of them, silhouettes of other escapees climbed along-side them. All of the others were faster. Every minute or two, someone younger and sprier had overtaken them, and Xueman had held Esther close as the faster folks passed them by without a word. Xueman had tied Rhonda's scarf around Esther's chest and had the other end wrapped around her fist, the old woman attached as tightly as David and the ice pick duct-taped to his forearm. That way she would be able to catch Esther every time the old woman stumbled and steady her every time she wobbled; she would be able to prod Esther along with a gentle tug whenever the old woman started to slow down. Esther would look at Xueman like she was a stranger who was holding open a door for her. The old woman had never called her by name.

On their second attempt, they had successfully made it to the top.

Just as when they had reversed the first time they tried their ascent, going down the other side of the wall was slower going than climbing up. Xueman went second, scared that Esther would slip and fall, but knowing that if she did and Xueman was below her, both of them would tumble off the wall. She let out a little length of Rhonda's scarf, acting like a safety lanyard on some mechanical elevator. Once, Esther had slipped, and it was only luck that Xueman had been able to wedge herself against a metal stand that had still held a few bags of chips from the quick mart that had once been a part of the strip mall. Esther had swung out like a pendulum over the white, suspended a moment over nothingness, like a soul hanging over the infinite void. Then Xue-man had pulled her back over to a ledge sticking out of the wall, and Esther had managed to grab hold.

Down. Down. Down. When Xueman's foot had finally touched snow, she almost dropped to her knees to kiss the ground. But she imagined her lips stuck to the frozen tundra and so remained on her feet.

Now Xueman stares into the white, searching for an end, looking for a face. Aspen's face. Instead of starting east, she makes her way along the edge of the exterior of the wall, back to the point approximately opposite of where the rest started up the inside of the barrier. Xueman searches the ground, looking for Aspen's footprints amongst a veritable stampede of feet. A lot of people had made it over the wall. Surely some will survive. So Roman's plan is working.

Is Aspen one of the survivors?

Of course, she is. Roman would not have let anything happen to her.

Xueman stares off into the white. Esther is at the end of the scarf, like a puppy on a leash, farther from the wall than Xueman. The old woman steps out into the white, almost disappearing in the veil even though Esther is still only an arm's span away.

"She looks just like you," Esther says, almost invisible in the white.

Aspen looks like a dream, unformed and more idea than person. It is the way Xueman first knew her, when a doctor had told the young single woman in the waiting room that she was pregnant. The person in her belly had been more thought than reality, a maybe that had not fully taken shape yet. Aspen appears from the white, faint and faded, before rushing in and snapping into place.

"Mom!"

The single greatest word in the world.

Aspen rushes into a mother's open arms. Xueman hugs her close, pulling her into an embrace that's been rare ever since her daughter had turned thirteen and eschewed most public displays of affection. Now, Aspen sobs against her shoulder like that newborn who had originally made Xueman's dreams a reality.

"Roman," Aspen chokes out.

Xueman pats her back. Now is not the time for details. Xueman urges them to get moving so they can get the hell off of this mountain.

Aspen takes her mother's hand, and they move east. Xueman holds Esther's hand as the three women make a human chain through the white.

"The rest?" Xueman asks, looking around. Shadows still scurry through the snow, flitting past and going, going, going. There are quite a few survivors. Then a shadow looms, the white turning gray. At first, Xueman flinches, putting herself between her daughter and danger. They say the thing in the white is a monster from the future, but Xueman is a woman of science. In medicine, the answer is never so far-fetched. Whatever it is, it will not keep Aspen from her own future. But the shape in the snow is not from the future, but a sentry of the present. An evergreen as tall as any science fiction creature. They move into the woods that mark the edge of town.

Aspen leads them through the trees, where the boughs break the wind and give them some shelter. Finally, Xueman recognizes a few survivors. Rhonda and the little girl appear out of the white. Trevin hugs himself against the cold, leaning alone against the trunk of a pine. But not all of them have made it over. Roman and David and Zack are all missing.

"The thing in the white took David, too," Aspen says, choking up again.

"David," Xueman sighs. "Damn it."

"We need to get the fuck away from that wall," Trevin states, as if he wants to change the subject from David's death. Denial. Survival.

"What about Zack?" Xueman presses, staring at Trevin. She should never have trusted Trevin with Zack. He was only using the boy as a shield.

Trevin looks back as Xueman stares at him. As if considering a lie. Out of kindness, to spare a terrible truth? Or to protect himself? Xueman has been a single mother now for eighteen years and possesses a finely tuned bullshit detector. She gives Trevin the same look she would give Aspen on many an occasion, the one that warned against telling a fib.

"Trapped," he confesses, a mother's glare more effective than a priest's collar or a vial of sodium pentothal. "The wall caved at the base of the wall. The monster was right there. I couldn't get him out."

Xueman takes Aspen by the hands, mittens in mittens. "I need to go back for him."

"You can't. It's too dangerous," Aspen pleads.

"He's trapped at the base of the wall. Just a few yards away. We can't just leave the kid behind."

"No," Aspen says. "He's just… He doesn't seem to want to live anyway."

"I don't let a patient die just because they do not care whether they live or not, Aspen. That isn't how it works."

"You always say that," Aspen cries. "But there are monsters in the white. The whole world isn't working like it is supposed to work, Mom."

"I love you, baby. You take Esther. Make sure she stays safe." Xueman passes the end of the scarf to her daughter, linking the old woman to Aspen. "Now I want you to run like hell."

Xueman turns without another word. Back toward the wall. The white swallows her up. The open space between the wall and the woods is maybe ten yards, but it seems like a mile. Forward, onward, the only thing in front of her is a wall. And maybe her untimely death.

She finds the wall, then moves along the base, shouting Zack's name over and over. She follows the perimeter of the wall, listening over the cry of wind. Xuemen is very aware that the monster might be anywhere.

She sees a glow within the gloom making shadows inside a cave created out of church debris.

Xueman pushes her face between some debris. "Zack?"

"Doctor Wang?" comes a muffled, surprised voice. "Is that you?"

"Let's get you out, Zack," she says, hefting a length of iron pipe sticking out from a section of destroyed drywall. She might weigh a hundred pounds and stand no taller than an average middle-schooler, but her size and weight could be offset by science. Physics trumps physicality. She makes a lever of the length of pipe and wedges it under the wreckage. Pushing against the frozen ground, she shifts a section to make a big enough gap that even the portly Zack can wriggle through between the snow and debris.

"You came for me," he says as he tugs himself out.

"Of course," Xueman answers, like there was never a question. "This way. Hurry!"

Xueman starts east, back to the woods. Another thirty feet and they would find shelter. The snow masks direction and everything is equal in the white. They are all one in the great blizzard of the world. The past is erased, the future an unformed wall of white, and possibility shifts with every bluster of wind. Moment to moment, she never knows if the white might part to reveal the way home or if the monster may come to steal her away.

Shadows shift. People are still coming over the wall and they scurry all around her. They come out of the snow and then disappear again. Xueman wants one of the shadows to solidify itself into her daughter, making the idea of her a reality again. She looks back every other step to make sure Zack is keeping up. Then there is a larger shadow than the rest, something bigger than just another person running, something coming rather than going.

Xueman stops, turns, and jumps without hesitation. She is not big enough to move Zack out of the way, so she jumps in front of him instead. The thing in the white reaches for the plump boy, but it snags Xueman Wang instead.

She is borne up, into the air, Zack right next to her at first, then disappearing by degrees. He is reaching up to her, screaming, but the words are carried away on the wind and delivered to someone else. Then he is erased, everything gone, just white, everywhere. Quiet. Peace. No wind and no snow. Just whitewhitewhitewhitewhite.

Then pain.

-38°

Rhonda pauses in the white. The shelter of trees is sporadic, a clustered copse blocking wind one moment and then a clearing that erases everything in the incessant snowstorm. Whirling all around, there is nothing in every direction. She has been lost in the blizzard before, wandering in circles, direction diffused so that east was everywhere and north was nowhere. Any direction she picks is right and wrong, getting them somewhere that would end up nowhere. Shadows appear in the curtain of snow, then disappear again, going this way and that. The periodic pines offer no detail, one evergreen like the next, covered with snow, white signposts with all the same message: *You're lost*. Outside the wall, without the demarcation of the buildings inside the town, there is no sense of west or south or even a straight line. Everyone darts through the white, desperate and directionless.

Trevin is on her right, staying close, his eyes sweeping the blizzard as if he thinks something is going to snag him at any moment. Something may. Aspen and Esther are on her left. Aspen had released Esther from the tether as soon as her mother had disappeared in the direction of the wall. She prefers holding the old woman's hand. Esther struggles through the storm, but Aspen will not let her flounder. She will drag her if she has to because Aspen made a promise to her mother.

Little Samantha clutches Rhonda tightly around the neck, the small girl sitting in the crook of her arm.

Rhonda had thought Aspen would insist that they wait for Xueman, but her mother had told her to run, and Rhonda has the sense that Aspen always listens to her mother. So as Rhonda plunged into the white, moving east, Aspen followed. They had all followed. But does Rhonda know where she's going? For so long, she has resisted moving forward, getting on, advancing in any way. Tomorrow is her birthday, and she has avoided it for the last fifty years. Now, she is trying to lead a whole group to tomorrow.

"We need to move faster," Trevin says coldly. "The old lady is slowing us down."

Rhonda glares at him through the white. "We leave no one behind."

"We left the doctor. We left Zack."

"She chose to go back. She told us to go on," Rhonda replies. "And *you* left Zack."

"Esther would want us to leave her behind, too."

"No one is stopping you from running off, Trevin. You can go ahead. There are plenty of other people running around in the white."

Then a large shadow moves along the ground, a mass that makes Rhonda shiver and shake. For a moment, she worries it is the wall, and they have circled back, not getting anywhere. Then she sees the shadow move and thinks that this is the end. The thing in the white has come to get her. But it is just a crowd, dozens of people moving as one. Several have phones, an image of a compass showing them east. Rhonda has been going in the right direction all along.

Amongst the crowd, carried with them like a snowflake on a breeze, is Zack, trudging downhill twice as fast as Rhonda and the others are moving. Esther *is* slowing them down, but Rhonda will never leave the old woman behind.

"Zack," Aspen shouts over the wind, letting go of Esther and rushing toward the boy.

Rhonda takes Esther's hand before the old woman forgets who she is supposed to be with and disappears into the stampede of people. Aspen catches Zack and brings him back into the fold. He glares at Trevin. The last of the original group returns, and the remaining survivors follow the swell of folks heading down the mountainside.

"My mother?" Aspen asks, although her tears reveal that she already knows the answer, freezing as soon as they fall, dashing to the snow like tiny diamonds.

Zack shakes his head. He looks like he wants to give the girl a hug, but he just walks along instead, inches between them that might as well have been miles. Aspen looks at the ground, leaving a trail of small icy beads. Esther surely does not remember her name, but she lets go of Rhonda's hand and takes the girl's again.

Like a snowball rolling down a hill, more and more survivors gather. Trevin looks back, meets Rhonda's eyes, then turns away. He moves forward with the tide of the crowd, disappearing into the white with other, *faster*, strangers. Then he is gone. The rest of them stay together, moving as one down the mountain, even as other escapees race by.

Around them, people disappear. Some scream as they are picked, plucked, pulled up and away into the white. Others go silently. Sometimes someone close to them pleads with a disinterested God as they reach up for someone as they are stolen away, as if they could pull them back from the thing in the white. Most are singular souls, appearing solo, disappearing alone, going into the sky without anyone to cry their names.

There are so many shadows around them, and even as one disappears here and there, dozens upon dozens remain. A large number of people seem to have attempted escape. Roman's plan worked. He did not survive, but he has given all these people a chance. They just had to get past the white. They just had to outrun the thing in the storm.

Then the blizzard is everything. The day starts to die. The white turns gray by shades. Rhonda stares into the snow, shifting, static, something amorphous that never takes shape. She expects the thing to be before her every step of the way, waiting, the monster right in front of her with an open mouth and a definite end. But each step, she survives.

She lives. She lives a little longer.

Zack collapses into the snow. One hand is missing a glove, has turned a purplish black, and is constantly tucked into his armpit. He lands with the arm caught under his considerable bulk. He struggles for a moment like a turtle tipped onto his back and then goes still.

"I can't," he huffs.

Aspen stops. She lets go of Esther, but Esther doesn't seem so lost. The old woman stays put. Aspen grabs Zack by his collar and pulls the big kid's head a few inches off the snowy ground, nose to nose.

"You will, God damn it," Aspen says. "My mother went back for you. So you better live, Zack. You better take the gift she gave you and fight for it. So get on your feet and get going, and I am not going to tell you again."

Zack struggles. Pulls out his hand that's more frost than flesh. He gets leverage and stands up. Tucks the popsicle into a pocket. Goes on. The next time he stumbles, he gets up on his own. Aspen does not have to tell him again.

Then there is something new in the graying white. Like the bloom of a bright yellow flower covered in a thin skin of frost. A tiger lily in the distance. Maybe Rhonda died and this is the light at the end of the tunnel? She turns to see if the others are still there. They are. She looks at Aspen to see if the girl sees what she sees. The bright yellow color of the thing in the distance catches in the icy beads sticking to Aspen's lashes. She sees. They all see.

The white stutters. Fades. With each step, they leave it behind. The yellow breaks up and becomes several eyes, all staring back as the white dissipates. It is a road, and dozens of vehicles in shallower snow are pointing headlights their way. Rhonda looks back, the yellow lamps reflecting off a wall of white stretching up into the sky like the face of a cliff. She stares, expecting the thing in the white to come out and reveal itself. But it doesn't. The horrors from the future remain hidden. Just more survivors, stragglers still struggling against the snow, coming out, outpacing the white.

Little by little, the wall of blizzard slips down the mountainside after them.

"C'mon," Rhonda says, turning her back on the snow. "It is time to get out of here."

As they get to the nearest truck, a kindly man with a great fuzzy beard reaches for Samantha. He reminds Rhonda of Roman. Rhonda gives the little girl over. Then she climbs up herself. She pulls Esther up beside her. Zack and Aspen get in the back. She sees Trevin riding shotgun in another vehicle, pulling away and pointing east.

It's over, she thinks as they drive away from the mountain.

Behind her, ponderous and relentless, the white follows.

-39°

Esther has not forgotten the people who have helped her survive the white: Rhonda. Aspen. Zack. She has not forgotten the friends who have fallen: Clarice. Xueman. Roman. David. A rare moment of clarity. As night falls on a day that she would like to forget, she remembers. There is so much to remember.

It was cold at the edge of the white. She had shivered uncontrollably as Rhonda led them through the blinding blizzard. Then the snow cleared, and for a while, it was just cold, and the white was gone. They were loaded into a pickup. Rhonda and the little girl and Aspen and Zack. The survivors.

The caravan stops at the bottom of Bailey's Peak. It is a small town overrun with hundreds of survivors. It is not snowing here, yet, and the roads are clear and passable. When Aspen opens the back door of the truck, the air is practically tropical. It feels like a summer breeze: the smell of sunshine and green grass and sandy beaches. Esther has not felt such warmth for as long as she can remember.

She did not know how cold she was until now.

Zack and Aspen stand side by side in the snow. The boy is twice her girth and blocks her from the direction of the mountain like a wall. Aspen does not look back. The day is too painful to face standing at the bottom of a mountain, waiting among strangers, just one among a flood of survivors who have all lost someone and something. The rest of her tears will thaw some warmer day.

Esther and the others are led into one of the small buildings along the perimeter. Someone with medical training comes along and looks over Esther. Her hands and feet are starting to hurt. Some of them, anyway. A few of her fingers and toes are still frozen. The woman has none of the tact of Xueman Wang and just wraps her in clean gauze, marks Esther with a number on a Post-it note, and moves on to Zack. She looks at Zack's frozen hand for a while, marks him with the same number as Esther, and finds other folks needing more immediate attention. Frostbite is not as immediate of an affliction as hypothermia.

Someone recognizes Samantha, still snuggled in Rhonda's arms. She claims to be a relation, and Samantha cries out "Auntie," and Rhonda gives her over. Samantha hugs the woman, who is crying and happy and sad, then the woman hugs Rhonda, who saved her precious niece. Rhonda saved Esther, too. She will have to remember to also give the woman a hug.

Trevin stands alone at the edge of the crowd of survivors. He ran. He left them. But it didn't matter. He could never have saved them. That thing in the white was horror in the flesh. Evil incarnate. A sentient force of death that was going to claim as many as it could. You cannot outrun the things that hide beyond the veil. Esther already knew that. She has been running ever since the first memory faded into white. There might be moments of clarity, but the sky always clouds again. The wind eventually stirs up the snow. And the white inevitability comes back, erasing everything.

"C'mon," Zack calls out to Trevin. "It's no time to be alone."

Trevin had left Zack behind. Zack is already willing to forgive. Leave the past behind him. Just as they left the future up in the mountain.

Trevin looks at the group. He doesn't belong with them. He doesn't belong anywhere. Esther might belong somewhere, but she will not remember where for long. She will forget Trevin and Aspen and Zack.

She will forget Rhonda. She will forget Roman. And Clarice. Eventually, even Walter will be erased by the white.

Trevin turns away from them. He doesn't answer Zack.

It hurts. Esther is starting to thaw. Her fingers and toes burn. The frosted flesh feels hot.

"How many people made it out?" Rhonda asks the local sheriff as the officer makes the rounds amongst the new batch of survivors. He is skittish, a man in over his head.

Walter always said to never trust a man who jittered too much. He either had to pee and postponed it, which made him imprudent, or he had something to hide, which made him suspicious.

Esther knows what the sheriff is hiding. He is scared out of his mind. So scared he might piss himself. That would make Walter doubly correct.

The cop's skin should be black, but it is as gray as hoarfrost, blanched by fear and denial. He has a beard like Roman's, wild and mangy, but his masks meekness, the kind of man who would have given up in the white. His eyes tell the tale. He is not a fighter. He is no Roman.

"You're the second wave of refugees," he says, fidgeting, eyes flitting out the large window facing west, up the steep slope. "The first group numbered thirty-eight survivors. Now you lot are another fifty-five. I sent more trucks and a pack of snowcats up the mountain."

"What happened?" Rhonda asks the officer. "What is going on up there?"

"It's not just up there," the sheriff says, his voice colder than the frost creeping at the edges of the window he looks through. "There are storm cells across the Midwest cutting off remote parts of Montana, North Dakota, Minnesota, Wyoming."

"This isn't the only place this is happening?" Trevin asks, approaching.

"No, son," the sheriff says, giving him a look that suggests that if Trevin is ready to run, the cop would run with him, lights on and sirens blaring. "Reports coming in from all over. More and more. Like an invasion."

"Are they really from the future?" Zack asks, as if he wants there to be a different explanation for what they saw.

"They tried to fix tomorrow," the cop says. "Instead, they broke today."

No one said anything. Another wave of survivors comes in. Three dozen more folks rescued from the white. That makes over a hundred refugees who successfully escaped from Zukunft Falls. Roman's plan had saved a lot of people. Esther has no doubt that by morning whoever stayed behind will be as dead as Walter and Clarice and What's-her-name and What's-his-name and the other What's-his-name. The new arrivals need room, so Esther and the others exit.

"Where do we go from here?" asks an obese teenager with scared eyes and a trembling mouth.

"Wherever we go, we go together," says a young Asian woman with sad eyes and a defiant grimace.

A young man with dark hair and a guilty gaze and an uncertain expression searches the crowd for another answer. Apparently finding nothing, he nods. "If you'll have me."

"Of course," answers the confident black woman with flint in her eyes and no bullshit in her mouth. "We'll stick together. I left a rented Expedition down at the pay lot in this town before I took a snowcat up the mountain to the resort. Let's get it and get out of here. Find a hospital. Someplace farther away from the white."

Her name is Rhonda, Esther remembers.

Forgetting is like the white. It really has no end. There is no place you can hide to avoid it. But Rhonda does not need to know that. None of them do. Even Esther doesn't need to know it. She forgets, nodding along with the rest of them. Away. That sounds nice.

The wind coming off the mountain turns colder. Esther shivers.

"I think we better be moving on," Esther says.

And the woman next to her smiles. Big and bright and a little too white. Esther cannot remember her name anymore, but she thinks maybe the black woman once helped her with something. She hugs herself against the cold. Whatever made her come to the mountains? A beach would be so much better.

The stranger takes her hand, some fingers unfeeling, others full of pins and needles. Esther plays along. It seems like she should know these people, so she just goes with it. Up the slope, a wall of white comes along on the back of the bitter wind.

The white is coming again.

ABOUT THE AUTHOR

Edward Newton won the Robert L. Fish Memorial Award for the Best First Short Story from the Mystery Writers of America. He has published numerous short stories. After an enlightening adventure exploring all of the contiguous United States, he has settled in sunny Florida.

Press
Presents

With barely a moment to rest after wrapping up his last case, Jasper O'Malley is handed another assignment that sends him and his partner, Amelia Rio, to the Big Apple. This time around Jasper's been hired to find a missing person, one Ray Armstrong, a former associate of his.

The trail eventually leads Jasper and Amelia into the tunnels beneath the city, where the case takes an unexpected turn when they stumble upon a desiccated corpse. As much as Jasper would like to believe there's a logical explanation for the condition of the body, all evidence points to one thing...

There's a vampire prowling the city and preying on its citizens.

Now, in addition to locating Armstrong, Jasper needs to track down and destroy the creature sucking the city dry in typical O'Malley style. God help New York City.

Midnight.

The Witching Hour.

But the creatures of darkness are not
confined to the shadows of the night.
Lonely stretches of highways…
Bustling college campuses…
Quiet suburban neighborhoods…
Pricey, upscale day spas…
They're everywhere.

Earl and Dale, a pair of burly truckers,
seem to be drawn to those that dwell in the darkness.
Monster hunters by default, they
confront the evil fearlessly—and with just a bit of humor.
Vampires, werewolves, half-human spider demons,
and those that prey on the innocent…
All will realize they've met their match
when they go head to head with…

The Midnight Men

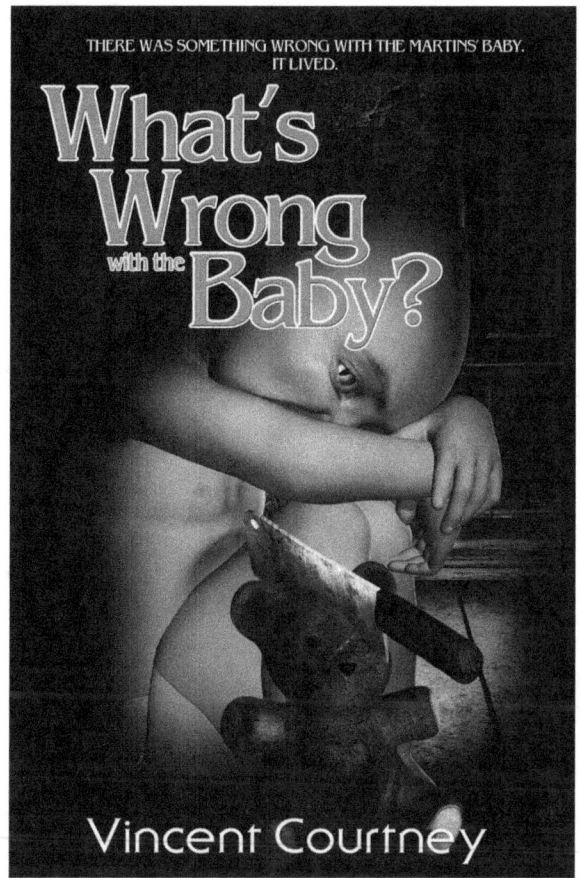

THERE WAS SOMETHING WRONG WITH THE MARTINS' BABY.
IT LIVED.

What's Wrong with the Baby?

Vincent Courtney

THE FEAR IS GROWING

From the moment he saw the ancient castle rising out of the picturesque Scottish countryside, filmmaker Dan Martin knew he'd found the ideal location for his vampire horror movie. And nothing could make him leave. Not the eerie legends of soul-stealing beasts of the night...nor a bizarre series of freak accidents. Not even his pregnant wife's tragic miscarriage.

THE TERROR IS BORN

Except that now there is another fetus growing in Vicki's womb. But little Darian is not going to be a normal baby. The Martins' adopted ten-year-old son Marty will soon find that out. In fact, Marty will soon know exactly what his new brother really is.

Shrouded in Mystery
The locals call it *Isla de los Perdidos*.
Island of the Lost.
According to the legends, those who venture onto the shores of
this cursed island never return.

Abandoned
Valarie DeNola and her sister Julie have chosen to ignore the
legends and the warnings. They have been selected to lead a team
of explorers to the island to discover the mystery surrounding it.
But once ashore, they become cut off from the outside world, and
what they discover is something they could never have prepared
for.

Inhabited by Death
Now they must fight against an unknown presence that is picking
them off one by one. No one can be trusted, and when even nature
rises up against them, all seems lost. Their one hope is the
extraction team they know is coming.

But will any of them survive to see it arrive?

If you can't run with the big dogs...

It was supposed to be a corporate retreat and a series of morale-boosting exercises. It was a weekend Shawn Biltmore nearly didn't survive.

There was something else playing in the woods that night, something other than a bunch of corporate drones with paintball guns.
And it had chosen Shawn as its new chew toy.

...rip 'em to shreds.

The local authorities chalked it up to a bear attack.
So did the doctors.
Shawn knew the truth, however, as much as he wanted to deny it.
But when one of his coworkers is viciously killed,
Shawn must face the truth...
He's a killer who needs to be put down.

Or is he?

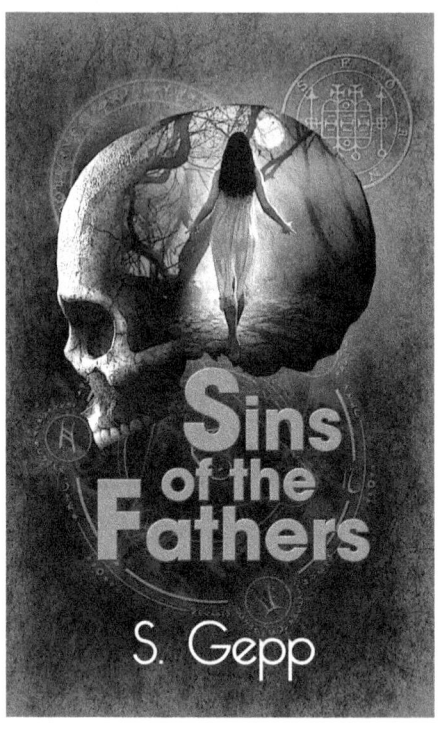

They called themselves The Round Table. Seven friends, a bunch of
nobodies in high school—until they learned the art of manipulation
and how much influence they could wield with the right bit of
knowledge. After years of being bullied, they had their first taste of
power…and they wanted more.

In college, they found their power had faded. Their petty blackmail
schemes no longer made others eager to do their bidding…and that
just wasn't acceptable. But the Darkness offered them everything
they could possibly want—for a price.
A price they were all too willing to pay.

And now, twenty-one years later, married with children and
successful careers, their past is coming back to haunt them and
threatening to take everything they hold dear. How much will they
lose before they can placate the spirit of the dead?

www.ingramcontent.com/pod-product-compliance
Lightning Source LLC
Chambersburg PA
CBHW060640260626
47161CB00008B/2938